NORTH TO MONTANA

When Buck Nation rides into Gunsight, he little knows what trouble awaits him. He has inherited the dilapidated Forty-Five ranch — but did its former owners really die in an accident? Questions mount, and Buck is bushwhacked. Is Selby Rackham, former cowhand at the Forty-Five and now the owner of the biggest spread around, somehow involved? With a woman, an old-timer and a scruffy dog as his allies, Buck is determined to smoke out the truth, whatever it takes . . .

COLIN BAINBRIDGE

NORTH TO MONTANA

Complete and Unabridged

LINFORD
Leicester

First published in Great Britain in 2013 by
Robert Hale Limited
London

First Linford Edition
published 2015
by arrangement with
Robert Hale Limited
London

A catalogue record for this book is available
from the British Library.

ISBN 978–1–4448–2282–3

Published by
F. A. Thorpe (Publishing)
Anstey, Leicestershire

Set by Words & Graphics Ltd.
Anstey, Leicestershire
Printed and bound in Great Britain by
T. J. International Ltd., Padstow, Cornwall

This book is printed on acid-free paper

1

The lone rider brought his horse, a blue roan gelding, to a halt. He took out his field glasses to take a closer look around. As he swept the rough terrain he could see nothing unusual. Yet he was convinced that something was not right. It wasn't just his own instincts that warned him of danger. The horse was sniffing the air as it shifted restlessly, its ears erect. He was sure that it could sense something, something unfamiliar and threatening. He put the glasses back into their holder and touched his spurs to the horse's flanks. He hadn't gone too much further when the worn frame buildings of the town of Gunsight came into view. The place looked a lot smaller than he had imagined. It certainly had a tired look about it. Well, if there were any answers to the questions that puzzled him, it was in Gunsight he would find them. He glanced about him once more before riding on.

The appearance of the town did not improve as he rode down the main street. There were few people about. He carried on till he saw a man sitting on a cane chair with its back propped against the wall of a dilapidated building. As he approached, he saw that the man was an old-timer. There was a dog lying at his feet. He drew the horse to a halt, swung down and tied it to a veranda rail.

'Be careful,' the old-timer said. 'If that horse skitters, the whole place is liable to come down.'

The stranger looked at the old man and then at the mangy dog lying at his feet, snoring.

'The dog got a name?' he asked.

'Sure,' the old-timer said. 'He's called Midway.'

'Funny name for a dog.'

'Called him after a remount station on the Pony Express route.'

'You rode for the pony express?'

The old-timer chuckled. He turned his head and spat. 'Nope, not me. Just helped out at the station. That was a job for youngsters. Nope, siree.' He glanced at the stranger and there was a reflective gleam in his eye. 'Elwood, Seneca, Marysville, Hollenberg.' He paused and seemed to draw himself together. 'I could go on,' he said, 'but I guess you got other things to do than listen to my ramblin's.'

The stranger looked up. 'Any place I can get supplies?' he said.

'There's old Ma Winslow at the grocery store. You could try her.'

The stranger nodded and turned away. He walked slowly down the street. The grocery store sign was splintered and flaked so much it was hard to read its faded letters. As he opened the door and pushed inside, a bell rang. A few moments later, a large, grey-haired lady emerged from the back. She peered at the new arrival through thick, horn-rimmed spectacles.

'I'll be needin' some things,' the stranger said.

While she was attending to his order, he glanced through the grimy window pane. The old-timer had tilted his chair back and seemed to have joined his dog in having forty winks. A few more people had appeared on the street. 'Things seem very quiet,' he remarked.

The old lady paused. 'Cholera,' she said. 'The place never got over it.'

'That why the graveyard seems so full?' he asked.

'You look on some of those headstones,' she replied. 'If you can still read 'em, that is. You'll see the year 1872 a lot. Those that don't carry the war years.'

'I already did,' he replied.

She put the last of his purchases in a bag. 'I haven't seen you around,' she said. 'Don't seem right friendly not to know your name.'

'Nation,' he said. 'Buck Nation.'

At the mention of his name, she started. 'Nation,' she repeated. 'Why, there's folk with that name in the graveyard.'

'Yeah,' he said. 'I noticed that too. But their gravestones weren't marked for 1872.'

'There used to be some folks by the name of Nation owned a little spread not far out of town. I think they used to call it the Forty-Five. You wouldn't . . .'

'Relatives,' he said. 'A different branch of the family.'

'I thought I didn't recognize you,' she said. 'Still, that wouldn't mean anythin'. Folks change, after all.'

'They do, ma'am,' he replied. 'They surely do.' Grabbing the parcel of groceries, he touched his hand to the brim of his hat and walked out the door. The bell jangled again and the woman stood motionless for a while before moving from behind the counter to the window. She peered outside. The sun was low in the sky and she put her hand to her eyes. When they had adjusted she saw the stranger riding away, his horse's hoofs kicking up dust. He seemed to be heading in the direction of the old Nation property.

Darkness had fallen by the time he came upon the remains of a broken-down sign which indicated that he was entering the old spread. The sign had once read 'Forty-Five', but it had faded and what was left of it looked like a noose. He continued to ride but the horse seemed agitated again. Its ears pricked and it grew skittish. Nation was alert to possible danger. A little further he waded through a shallow stream and then, seeing the looming shape of the ranch-house ahead of him, dropped from the saddle and knee-haltered the horse. It was tossing its head and Nation decided he would go the rest of the way on foot.

He drew his six-gun and began to move stealthily forward. As he expected, the place was deserted. He crept through the yard and stepped onto the dilapidated veranda of the ranch-house. The door had swung open and he was about to step inside when he suddenly froze in his tracks. He thought he had heard a sound. He flattened himself against the

6

wall, holding his gun at the ready. There was a quiet moment, and then a crashing in the brush. From among the trees a dark form, huge and cumbersome, lumbered into the open.

Nation raised his gun and fired towards it, but the last vestiges of daylight had faded and the moving shadows were deceptive. It seemed he must have missed because the next moment the dark mass was upon him, growling, snarling and smelling foul. Nation realized it was a grizzly bear and the gunshot had made it furious. Like a doll he was bowled over, but he managed to roll aside and stagger to his feet. The bear turned and reared up on its hind legs. Nation had dropped the gun and faced it now with his knife in hand. The bear was roaring and gnashing its teeth. Foam flew from its mouth and dribbled down its face and neck.

Not waiting for it to attack, Nation seized the initiative and rushed in, attempting to drive his knife into its stomach. With a roar the animal swiped at him and Nation felt the sharp claws tear across his chest. As the bear closed in, attempting to squeeze him, he sprang back. He lifted the knife once more but it had snapped. The bear dropped to four legs, and as it rushed at him Nation took to his heels, heading towards the stream. He plunged in and waded to the opposite side. The bear came charging after him but as it approached the water it veered away and went lumbering back into the undergrowth.

Nation looked down at his chest. His thick sheepskin coat had saved him from serious damage, but the grizzly's razor-sharp claws had slashed through the material and there was a bad cut across his chest. He waited for several minutes before wading back into the stream and splashing the icy cold water over his wound. It was quite deep and bleeding badly. He came out of the water and cautiously began to make his way to where he had left the roan. He felt fairly sure that it was the presence of the bear which he had sensed on his way into Gunsight and which had so alarmed his horse. Maybe there was more than one of them in the neighbourhood.

He soon reached the horse and felt in his saddle-bags. He always carried some basic medical supplies and he bound up the wound as best he could. He had suffered worse and at least it did not seem to affect any movement in his arm. So far he had not opened the flask of whiskey he carried, but now he took a long swig. The liquid coursed through his body and he felt better. He had intended staying in the ranch-house but, with the bear around, it was too dangerous and he resolved to find somewhere else to make camp.

By the time he had found a suitable spot at a safe distance from the Forty-Five, his chest hurt badly but the bleeding had stopped. He rubbed down the horse and fed it with corn the woman back in town had provided.

Using bark, leaves and dry branches he soon had a small fire blazing among some rocks. He filled the kettle with icy water from a brook to make coffee. It tasted good. Firelight flickered and danced and reflected from the rocks, providing warmth as well as a deterrent to any hostile wildlife. Somewhere nearby a hoot owl called its lament. From time to time the horse snickered or stamped. He lay his head against his saddle and tried to sleep but the pain in his shoulder seemed to be growing worse. The night was well advanced before he finally managed to fall into a troubled slumber.

Something large with burning eyes was pursuing him. He strained every sinew to escape but no matter how fast he tried to run, he made no progress. He could not get away from whatever was behind him. He felt its hot breath on his neck and he awoke with a start to find an amorphous shape looking down on him. He tried to move but a wave of pain engulfed him and he fell back into a yawning abyss which yet somehow seemed oddly comforting. His head throbbed and he felt as though he was burning. He heard a droning in his ears, which he slowly realized was someone's voice.

'How are you feelin'?' the voice said. 'Not so good, I guess.'

He opened his eyes again and the amorphous shape began to condense and take on features. It was the grizzled face of an old man. It looked vaguely familiar. He struggled to remember and then he realized it was the old-timer he had met when he first rode into town.

'Take another sip of this,' the old-timer said. He held a flask to Nation's lips and tipped it gently. Nation took a few sips but most of it got spilled. 'I got somethin' stronger,' the old-timer added, 'but right now I figure water's what you need.'

Although he hadn't swallowed much, Nation began to feel a little improved. He began to take cognizance of his surroundings. He seemed to be in the same place he had set up camp. It was daylight but he still felt cold inside his sheepskin coat. Summoning up some reserve of strength, he succeeded in sitting up.

'What are you doin' here?' he asked.

'Just as well I came by,' the old-timer replied. 'Fact is, I felt kinda guilty. I should have warned you about that bear. He's been causin' trouble 'round these parts for quite a time. When I didn't see you come back to town, I figured you might have run into the varmint. So I rousted out my old mule and took a ride to the Forty-Five. It didn't take me long to figure out what happened.'

Nation was beginning to feel better. 'Did you say you had somethin' stronger in your saddle-bags?' he asked.

The old-timer's face creased into a toothless grin. 'Sure have,' he said. He walked away to where the mule was standing and returned in a few moments with a flask in his hand which he handed to Nation, who took a sip and then gasped.

'Hell,' he said. 'What you got in there?'

'It's my own recipe,' the old-timer replied. 'Mainly raw alcohol, but with a few extra ingredients thrown in.'

'What ingredients?'

'Liquid coffee, burned sugar, chewin' tobacco, red pepper.'

Nation took another swig. His throat burned and his eyes felt as though they were popping out of his skull. All the same, once he had recovered from the initial effects, he had to admit it made him feel a whole lot better.

'By Jiminy,' he said, 'I ain't felt anythin' burn like that before.'

'That'll be the creosote,' the old-timer replied.

Nation handed the flask back. 'Leave some for the bear,' he said. 'It'll sure fix him once and for all.' He struggled to his feet. For the first time he realized that his chest had been bandaged. 'Did you do that?' he asked.

'It should work,' the old-timer replied. 'I packed some salt pork in there to help stop any infection.'

'You've worked as a doctor as well as with the pony express?' Nation asked.

The old-timer disregarded any trace of irony. 'You remembered?' he replied. 'I ain't got no diploma, if that's what you mean, but I picked up a few tips along the way. In fact I used to run a medicine show one time. That's a patented medicine you just swallowed.'

Nation looked down at his chest. 'Well, I guess I owe you,' he said. 'Sure appreciate what you done. Say, we haven't been properly introduced yet. The name's Nation, Buck Nation.' He held out his hand and the old-timer took it. His hand felt like the rough bark of a tree.

'Glad to make your acquaintance,' he said. 'Folks call me Muleskin.'

'I take it that ain't your proper name?'

'I guess maybe not, but I've had it so long I plumb forget bein' called anythin' else.'

Nation glanced around. 'Hey, where's the dog?' he said.

'Midway?' Muleskin replied. 'I left him behind this time. He's gettin' kinda old like me. He'll be wonderin' where I've got to.' He looked at Nation. 'If you like, you could come back with me. I wouldn't advise goin' too far just yet, not till that wound has healed some.'

Nation considered his invitation. It made a lot of sense. The old-timer was right; he wasn't really in a fit condition to carry on straight away. He had business with the old Forty-Five ranch, but he was operating in the dark. Maybe he could pick up information in Gunsight. Muleskin might know something. He remembered the way the old lady in the general store had reacted to the mention of his name. If it stirred any reaction in Muleskin, he certainly hadn't shown it.

'That's mighty nice of you,' he said. 'Just so long as I won't be causin' you any bother.'

Muleskin grinned and spat out a long jet of phlegm. 'No bother at all,' he

15

said. 'In fact, I'll be glad of some company.'

Nation began to remove the traces of his camp. Muleskin moved towards the mule and as he did so, Nation noticed for the first time that he walked with a pronounced limp. When they were ready, they mounted up — Nation on the roan and Muleskin on his mule. Then they set out towards Gunsight.

It wasn't a lengthy journey, but to Nation, in his depleted state, it seemed to take a long time. It came as a relief when he saw some shacks ahead of them which indicated that they were almost there. Now that they were near, he felt he owed it to the old-timer to check that he hadn't changed his mind about putting him up.

'Like I said,' Muleskin replied, 'I'd be honoured to have you. That place you saw me outside of yesterday used to be the Broken Wheel saloon. The lady who ran it still lives there. She gives me room.'

Nation considered his words for a

moment. 'Maybe she'll object to some-body turnin' up out of nowhere.'

Muleskin laughed and spat again. 'Hell no,' he spluttered. 'You don't have to worry about that. The place is too big for us both. We just rattle around in there like two old peas in a pod, a large pod. We hardly see each other from one day to the next.'

'What's she called, this lady?' Nation asked.

'Don't rightly know that either, not for sure,' he replied. 'She was always known as Annie: Double-Cinch Annie.'

'Funny name.'

'Yeah, I suppose so. Ain't gave it any thought. That old saloon could get mighty rowdy. Guess she always man-aged to stay in control.'

They had reached the main street of town. To Nation's eyes it seemed slightly bigger than on his first impress-sion, and there were more people about. As they clattered by, a few faces were turned in their direction. They came to a halt outside the old saloon and tied their horses to the hitch rack.

'There's room out in the yard,' Muleskin said. 'I'll take 'em round later.'

As they mounted the steps to the boardwalk, there was a sudden commotion and through the faded batwing doors the dog came scampering. He ran to Muleskin and jumped up at him, then dashed backward and forwards, falling over as he did so.

'Good boy, Midway,' Muleskin said.

Nation bent down as the dog turned its attention to him, its tongue lolling out, and tickled it behind the ear. 'That's a nice welcome,' he said. He noticed that, like its master, the dog was limping slightly and there was a big swelling on its left leg.

'He's an old fella now,' Muleskin said, 'but he does all right.' With the dog at their heels, they stepped through the batwings.

Nation looked around. What must have once been the saloon had been transformed into a parlour. The plush furnishings had faded; a mirror still remained, along with a massive chandelier. There were other indications that the place had once served quite a different function and the effect was oddly disconcerting.

'Neither of us uses this part any more,' Muleskin said. 'Annie has most of the top floor and I got a place out back.'

He led the way through a doorway into the room beyond. There was a bed and some shelves, a couple of chairs and a table — but not much else apart from a battered, rusty stove. Through a grimy window Nation could see a yard with a tumbledown shack in one corner, which he guessed comprised the stabling to which the old-timer had referred.

'Kinda strange the place has no front door,' Nation remarked. 'Anyone could walk in.'

Muleskin shrugged. 'It don't happen,' he said, 'but it wouldn't matter anyway. Annie's quarters are private and there's nothin' here a body would waste time tryin' to steal.'

Nation glanced round the room and back through the door at the parlour. 'I guess not,' he replied.

The old-timer looked down at Midway. 'He's done his time as a guard dog,' he added, 'but he's kinda retired now, just like me.' He stroked the dog's head. 'Come through here,' he said. 'This'll be yours.'

He led the way to a room beyond, which was dusty with lack of use. An old bunk stood in a corner. 'I ain't sayin' it's a palace,' he said, 'but I figure you've probably seen a lot worse.'

The old-timer was right, on both counts. 'It's fine,' Nation replied. 'Anyway, I don't figure on stayin' for long.'

Muleskin gave him a quizzical look. 'Stay just as long as you like,' he said. 'Get your stuff out of your saddle-bags and I'll stable those animals and fix somethin' to eat.'

He turned and went out of the room, followed by the dog. Nation looked about him once more. There had been no further mention of Double-Cinch Annie and he wondered when he was likely to meet her.

A day went by. Nation had no intention of outstaying his welcome, but, although he didn't like to admit it, he wasn't feeling too good. Muleskin helped him change the bandages on his chest; the wound seemed to be healing OK but it had obviously affected him. By the evening, however, he was feeling better and in need of some air.

'I'm gonna take a little stroll,' he said.

'There ain't a lot to see,' Muleskin replied. 'Figure you'll about cover it by the time I got some coffee brewed.'

'I hope it ain't anythin' like your notion of whiskey,' Nation responded.

He went through the parlour and out of the batwings. The night was cool. The street was deserted; scattered lamps showing in the windows only served to emphasize the sense of desolation which enveloped the town. Nation paused before continuing till he saw ahead of him a low mound over which hung a sign. He had already stopped by on his way into Gunsight. It was the town cemetery. He paused at the entrance before turning and starting to climb the rise. The moon hung low behind it and the dim shapes of crosses were etched against the skyline.

Stopping beside one of them, he bent down to read the name: Cliff Nation. Nearby, a second cross was marked with the name of Henrietta Nation. It seemed strange that he and they shared the same blood, though they had never met and he hadn't even known they existed until a few short weeks before. He still didn't know much about them, but Muleskin might be able to supply him with further details. There was no time like the present. Muleskin would have coffee bubbling on the stove; it would be a good time to talk with him.

He turned to go. At the same moment he heard the crack of a rifle behind him and a bullet thudded into the wooden cross. If he hadn't moved, he would have been hit. Diving to the ground, he rolled away from the cross and suddenly found himself falling. He landed with a jarring thud which knocked the wind from him. He lay for a moment looking up at the sky, which was framed in a dark rectangle. He was in a cramped position and when he tried to move he found it difficult. He succeeded in sitting up and then he realized that he had fallen into an open grave. In the darkness he had not even seen it.

His thoughts were interrupted by a second shot. He drew his six-gun and struggled to his feet. His head rose just above the edge of the grave and he peered about. He could see nothing but he heard the unmistakable snarling of a dog. It was followed by another gunshot and then the sounds of a scuffle taking place at the entrance to the graveyard. He heard the whinny of a horse followed by the rapid castanet of hoofs. He looked upwards. The hoof-beats were coming from the direction of the road he had walked along, but they were travelling quickly away from town. In another few seconds they had dwindled away into the night. Placing his gun back in its holster, with some difficulty he hauled himself out of the pit.

His injured chest hurt. He stood and looked about him but he was alone. His clothes were grimy and he wiped them down with his Stetson before moving quickly forward, puzzling over what could have happened to frighten off his attacker. As he emerged from the graveyard he saw a dark shape lying in the road and he knew instantly that it was the dog, Midway. He remembered the gunshot and ran forward, fearful of what he might find. He kneeled down and to his immense relief saw that the dog was still breathing. He could see no obvious injury and after a few moments the dog roused itself and struggled to its feet. It stood, looking up at him, with its tongue lolling.

'Good boy,' he said, stroking it under

the chin and wondering who could have taken the shot at him. Nobody knew of his presence in Gunsight. At least, so he had thought. 'Come on, old fella,' he said, 'let's get you home.' He started to walk slowly away and the dog followed in his footsteps.

When he got back, although the night was chill, Muleskin was sitting outside at the back of the building. A wide porch gave access to a yard and the decrepit outhouse which passed muster as the stable. Muleskin showed some surprise at seeing the dog tagging along behind.

'I've topped up the coffee pot,' he said. 'Hope it ain't too weak now. I already had a mug.' He poured the thick black liquid. Nation sat in a chair and took a drink. It didn't affect him quite like the old-timer's whiskey but it wasn't far short.

'I hope Midway ain't been causin' you any bother,' Muleskin continued. 'He sure seems to have taken to you.'

The dog had settled between the two

of them. Nation reached down and patted its head.

'Just the opposite,' he said. 'I got Midway to thank for helpin' save my life.'

Muleskin looked at Nation with an expression of enquiry on his grizzled features.

'I took a walk to the cemetery,' Nation explained. 'While I was there somebody bushwhacked me. I was in a real fix till the dog decided to take a hand. Whoever it was, he drove him off.'

'Well, I'll be!' Muleskin exclaimed.

'One shot was probably aimed at Midway but I can't see any damage.'

Muleskin bent down and, holding the kerosene lamp in his hand, examined the dog.

'There's a burn mark,' he said. 'Hell, he's got so many old scars and marks it's kinda hard to tell, but I figure this is a new one.'

Nation took a look. There was a singe along the dog's side. 'That was close,' he said. 'Hey, I'm sorry about Midway, but I didn't know he was there. He musta followed me.'

'Sounds like it was a good job he did,' Muleskin replied.

Nation reached into his shirt pocket and drew out his muslin sack of Bull Durham with its packet of brown papers attached. He quickly rolled a cigarette and then passed the sack to the old-timer. They lit up and took another swallow of coffee before Muleskin resumed the conversation.

'I don't understand why anyone would take a shot at you,' he said. 'Nobody knows you around these parts.'

'That's what I was tryin' to figure,' Nation replied. 'Whoever it was, he must have been watchin' me.'

Muleskin looked out into the night. 'Maybe I'd better turn down the lamp,' he said. He fumbled for a moment and dimmed it. 'You never know,' he added. 'This back porch is pretty secluded, but there's no point in takin' chances.'

'I can't figure it out,' Nation repeated.

Muleskin looked at him. 'It ain't none of my business,' he said, 'but maybe it'd be an idea if you were to tell me a bit more about what you're doin' here in Gunsight.'

Nation blew out a ring of smoke. 'It is your business now,' he said. 'Especially after what Midway just did for me. Besides, I was meanin' to ask you a few questions myself. Maybe you can help.' He paused to finish his coffee before resuming.

'I'll keep it short,' he continued. 'A couple of weeks ago I was contacted by a certain Justin Delaney. He's an attorney-at-law. He wrote that if I was to contact him at his offices in Kansas City, I might find somethin' to my advantage. I was goin' to ignore him. I wasn't even sure if it was me his letter was aimed at. But in the end I went along and paid him a visit. I didn't like the looks of him, but that's beside the point. He asked me for some proof of who I was and then he told me that I'd been left a ranch called the Forty-Five in the neighbourhood of a town called Gunsight in Wyoming territory. I figured the whole thing was probably some kinda hoax but he assured me it was all legal and above board.'

'He must have persuaded you to his way of thinkin' or you wouldn't be here. It's quite a ways from Kansas City to Wyoming.'

'Maybe I just had nothin' better to do. Anyway, I figure you've been around these parts for a long time. Do you know anythin' about the Forty-Five?'

The old-timer shook his head. 'A bit, not much. A man called Cliff Nation and his wife, Henrietta, used to run it but they kept pretty much to themselves. They'd come into town from time to time for supplies but nobody knew them too well. As far as I know, they both died in an accident. They were out ridin' and their buggy turned over.'

'An accident? That's interestin'.'

'The marshal was happy about it. I mean, there was no suspicion of foul play, if that's what you're thinkin'.'

'Why would I think that?' Muleskin didn't reply so Nation continued: 'The marshal? Has the town got a marshal?'

'Not any more. But it used to be bigger and livelier in those days. That was before the cholera and before the cattle herds moved on.'

'What was his name? Is he still around?'

'Rice Quitman? Sure. He's retired now. Has a nice little place just outa town. I could take you there to meet him.'

'That might be a start,' Nation replied. 'What about the rest of the folks in town? Do you reckon any of them might be able to throw light on the matter?'

'You could ask around. I doubt whether any of 'em would know much more than me. Have a word with Doc Hurley.'

'OK. That's another call I'll make tomorrow,' Nation replied. He got to his feet. 'Well,' he said, 'if it's OK with you, I guess I'll turn in now.'

'Me too,' Muleskin replied. 'It's gettin' a mite chilly. There's a cold wind comin' off the mountains.'

They moved indoors and Nation noticed again how badly the old man limped. He went through to the inner room and threw himself down on the bunk. He closed his eyes. The last thing he heard before sleep claimed him was the sound of snoring, but whether it was the old-timer or his dog he would have been hard put to say.

2

Early the next morning, having arranged with Muleskin to ride out to see the former marshal later in the day, Nation went to talk with the doctor. As he entered the house, a figure emerged from some inner recess.

'Howdy,' Nation said.

The doctor was a small, lean man with a thin moustache. 'Can I be of assistance?' he asked.

'Yes, I'm hopin' you might be able to help me. The name's Nation, Buck Nation. I got some relatives buried up at the cemetery.'

'Nation,' the doctor repeated. 'You mean, you're related to Cliff and Henrietta Nation who used to run the old Forty-Five?'

'Yeah, although I didn't know it till recently.' In a few clipped words he told the doctor something of his story. 'Can you tell me anythin' about them or how they died?' he concluded.

'Sorry. I never really knew them personally, but they were well respected in Gunsight. I understand they were tragically killed in an accident when their buggy overturned.'

'So the story goes,' Nation replied. 'By the way, I also noticed an open grave.'

The doctor eyed him quizzically. 'There's nothin' unusual about that. Old Tom likes to keep ahead of things.'

'Old Tom?'

'Tom Irwin. He's a kind of general handyman. He works for me sometimes.'

'Well,' Nation said, 'that doesn't get us far.' He exchanged glances with the doctor. 'After what happened last night, I almost got a feelin' like that grave was meant for me. Anyway, thanks for your help.'

'Where are you going now?'

'To see the former marshal. Maybe he can tell me somethin' about Cliff

33

and Henrietta's accident.'

Nation and the doctor made their way back into town, where they parted. When Nation arrived at the old saloon, Muleskin already had their mounts saddled and ready to go. This time the old-timer was riding a dappled grey mare.

'Not ridin' your mule today?' Nation asked.

'The old girl's gettin' slower, like me and Midway. Figured I'd give her a break.'

Before mounting they stood for a moment, looking up and down the street.

'What did the doc say?' Muleskin asked.

'Only that nobody has died so far as he's aware.'

'So whose grave was it you found?'

'Nobody's yet,' Nation replied. 'The doc told me that the gravedigger likes to keep on top of things.'

'Tom Irwin? Yeah, that would figure. He's a good man. This town don't amount to much, but I figure it would have fallen down altogether without him.'

They mounted up and set off down the main street. The town still wore its customary hangdog look, but Nation was beginning to get more used to it. He had been in worse places.

The ride out to see the former marshal took longer than Nation had expected. They were heading towards the broken hills beyond which the higher ranges reared into the sky.

'Watch for that bear,' Muleskin said. 'I reckon he's made the foothills his territory.'

'Is he some kind of rogue?' Nation replied.

'There have certainly been a few incidents,' the old-timer replied. 'Not just recently, though, apart from the attack on you.' He spat. 'Goddamned bears!' he said, with emphasis. 'I don't like 'em. I'll get that son of a bitch sometime.'

'I guess he was only doin' what a

bear does,' Nation replied. 'I figure leave 'em alone so long as they leave you alone.'

'That's just what that critter ain't been doin'. And he isn't the worst, not by a long way. Someday . . . ' Muleskin stopped. He was almost gasping and Nation was startled to see his features distorted by rage. Suddenly he had an intuition about how the old-timer had acquired his limp.

'You got a particular reason to hate 'em?' he said, half-questioning and half-making a statement. Muleskin rode on without replying but after a short distance drew his horse to a halt.

'You're right, Nation,' he said. 'I got good reason to hate the varmints. You seen the way I walk. Well, I got that limp from a bear, up in those mountains. One day I'm goin' back and take revenge. One day his head's gonna be hangin' on a nail.'

Nation didn't say anything. He was still taken aback by the vehemence of Muleskin's outburst. It didn't seem to chime with the impression he had formed of the old-timer. Eventually Muleskin seemed to calm down a little.

'Hell, guess you're wonderin' what's got into me,' he said. He looked up again at the higher ranges. 'Come on, let's ride. We've still got a few miles to go.'

'You sure you're OK?' Nation said.

'Sure. I guess I've let that old grizzly plumb get under my skin.'

Without waiting for a reply, Muleskin dug his spurs into the grey's flanks and rode forwards. Nation followed suit. That bear did more than just wound the old fella physically, he thought. Maybe there's more to this than he's lettin' on.

The former marshal's house was set beside a grove of trees with a stream rippling through. It was a pleasant spot, somewhat isolated — but the kind of place a man, happy enough in his own company, might choose. Or a man trying to escape from something. As they tied their horses to the hitching rail, the door opened and the former marshal stepped out onto the porch.

'Muleskin,' he said. 'It's good to see you.' His eyes fell on the old-timer's companion.

'Quitman, this is Buck Nation,' Muleskin said. 'He's a friend of mine.'

Quitman shook Nation's hand. 'Come on in,' he said. 'I reckon you wouldn't say no to some refreshment after comin' this far.'

He led the way inside and while Nation and Muleskin made themselves comfortable, he poured the contents of a decanter into three tumblers.

'An Irish import,' he said. He turned to Nation. 'Since you're still here with us, I take it you haven't yet sampled Muleskin's own recipe?'

Nation laughed. 'Matter of fact I have,' he replied. 'Only there were mitigatin' circumstances.'

'He'd just been attacked by a bear,' Muleskin put in.

Nation looked across at him. 'Come

to think of it,' he said, 'I'm not sure which was worse.'

It was Quitman's turn to laugh. 'I hope you're on the way to recovery,' he said.

Nation nodded, although he wasn't feeling too good. 'Still hurts some, but it'll be fine. Thanks to Muleskin.' He felt that some explanation of his presence was needed and he proceeded to give the former marshal an indication of what he was doing in Gunsight, concluding with what had happened since his arrival.

When he had finished the former marshal was thoughtful. He rubbed his hand across his chin.

'So you're now the owner of the Forty-Five,' he said. 'I didn't know that Cliff Nation and Henrietta had any family.'

'Neither did I till I heard from that attorney,' Nation replied.

'I'm tryin' to think back to the accident,' Quitman said.

'Where did it happen?' Nation asked.

'Was it somewhere on the Forty-Five?'

'Nope. It wasn't far out of town. I assumed Cliff and Henrietta had been on their way to town to pick up supplies or maybe just have a run out. They used to do that sometimes. Their buggy was found overturned with the pair of them underneath it.'

'Do you know who found them?'

'Sure. It was young Duane Gunter.' He turned to the old-timer. 'You remember him, Muleskin? He often helped out at the Forty-Five.'

'I remember him,' Muleskin replied.

'Is he still livin' in Gunsight?' Nation asked.

'Nope,' Quitman replied. 'I think he left town not long after the accident. He shows up from time to time, but I ain't seen him in a while.'

'So what happened to the Forty-Five?'

'Nothin' much. The cattle were sold off and then it was left to go to rack and ruin. I don't know why. It weren't much of a place, I guess.' He suddenly recollected that Nation was now the owner. 'Sorry, I never meant . . . '

'It's OK,' Nation replied. He paused for a moment before asking the question which was uppermost in his mind. 'I don't know how to put this, but, lookin' back, are you quite sure that Cliff Nation and Henrietta died as the result of an accident?'

'What do you mean?'

'Don't get me wrong. I'm just feelin' my way. Somebody took that shot at me, so there's obviously more to this whole business than meets the eye. There's somethin' goin' on and it's connected in some way with the Forty-Five and what happened in the past.'

'Well, I didn't have any reason to think otherwise,' Quitman said. 'If there had been anythin' suspicious, I think I would have noticed it. Nope, I think you're barkin' up the wrong tree there.'

'There wouldn't have to be any obvious signs,' Muleskin said, 'but somethin' must have happened to skitter their horse. It could have been done deliberately.'

Quitman shrugged. 'I suppose you've got a point,' he said. 'But if that was the case, if someone did it on purpose, they wouldn't be likely to leave any evidence.'

They sat in silence for a moment. Nation picked up his glass and finished the rest of his whiskey.

'Well, I don't know where this leaves things,' he concluded, 'but I sure appreciate your help.'

They continued to talk but when the time came to leave, Nation had the feeling that he hadn't made much progress. As they mounted up, the former marshal addressed Muleskin.

'Say, I forgot to ask about Midway. How's the old fella doin'?'

'Same as usual,' Muleskin replied.

'Bring him along next time,' Quitman said.

Nation looked back as they rode away. The former marshal remained standing on the porch. It was then that it struck him that Quitman had enquired after the dog but hadn't mentioned Double-Cinch Annie. Was there something odd in that? It seemed more likely that he would have enquired after both of them rather than one and not the other. But then, he had only referred to the dog as an afterthought. There was probably nothing in it.

As they rode back to Gunsight, Nation began to feel unwell. Muleskin couldn't help but notice the way he slumped over the saddle.

'Are you feelin' OK?' he asked. Nation shook his head. 'You've been overdoin' things,' the old-timer responded. 'It's only a day since that bear varmint attacked you. There's poison in a bear's claws. You'd better rest easy when we get back. Maybe you should have mentioned it to the doc. I'll get him to come over and take a look at you.'

As far as Nation was concerned, it seemed to take an age to cover the last leg of the journey back. When he and Muleskin reached town he was feeling really bad but did his best to sit upright in the saddle and not show it. The old-timer helped him from his horse and then through the batwing doors to his own room. Nation was about to remonstrate with him about being given his mattress but he couldn't fight his exhaustion any longer; he would have collapsed had not Muleskin caught him and laid him on the bed. He dimly heard his voice telling him to lie still before blackness came over him.

When he came to, he didn't know where he was. Then slowly his senses returned and he recognized the old-timer's room. He was covered in a clean sheet and blankets, and his throbbing head was propped on a mound of pillows. It was dark, the only illumination coming from a shaded lamp. He became aware that someone else was in the room with him. Wincing with the effort, he turned his head, expecting to see Muleskin, but to his surprise it was a woman. She was dressed in a faded purple gown and her hair was arranged in a huge chignon. She smiled at him.

'Well, Mr Nation,' she said, 'it seems like you've pulled through at last. How are you feeling now?'

'Not too bad. My head hurts.'

'That isn't surprising. At least you're past the worst. How about your chest? Some of those scars were quite deep.'

He looked down to see that his chest was freshly bandaged. 'It feels fine,' he said. 'Maybe a little bit sore.' He glanced round. 'Where's Muleskin? I didn't mean to take his bed. He'll be needin' it.'

'Just lie still. Muleskin is asleep. I would have transferred you to one of the rooms upstairs but it didn't seem to be worth disturbing you.'

'I'd best get up. I'm fine now. A few hours' rest is all I needed.' The woman's previous words suddenly registered with him. 'Say, how long have I been lying here?' he said.

'Two days.'

'What time is it?'

'Four in the morning. It'll soon be dawn.'

'I didn't mean to inconvenience any-one.'

'It's no inconvenience. In fact, I'm

glad to have been able to be of some help. We don't get too many visitors. This town isn't exactly the kind of place anyone goes out of their way to stop by.'

'Would I be correct in assumin' you're Annie?'

'I am indeed. Annie McGrew. And you're Buck Nation. Muleskin has told me something about your circumstances.'

'I owe Muleskin. And now it seems I owe you too, but don't worry. Just as soon as I can get saddled up, I'll be on my way.'

He made to get out of bed but Annie restrained him. 'You may be over the worst,' she said, 'but you're in no fit state to be going anywhere. Just take it easy. I guess you could probably do with something to eat? I'll rustle up some grub.'

She got to her feet and walked out of the room, her skirts swishing as she did so. Nation struggled to an upright position. He looked through the window. The sky was still black and it was suddenly borne in on him that she must have been sitting up with him all night. Before long she was back, carrying a tray on which stood a bowl of broth and some bread.

'Here, try this,' she said. 'Later, you can maybe have something more substantial.'

He spooned some of the broth into his mouth. It tasted good and, when he had finished, he already felt strengthened. As he did so he observed the woman more closely. He guessed that she was in her early fifties. Her yellow hair was streaked with grey and there were crow's feet lines about her eyes. She must once have been quite a beauty and she was still a good-looking woman with a figure he couldn't help admiring.

'Thanks again,' he said when he had finished. 'I sure appreciate everythin' you and Muleskin have done for me.'

She rose to take away the bowl and spoon. 'I'll leave you now,' she said. 'Try and get some more rest. As for those other matters, we can decide what's to be done next in the morning.'

She turned down the lamp and went out the door but Nation remained looking through the window, thinking over what she had said. There was something comforting about her words, as if she was on his side, as if already there was some kind of understanding between them. She seemed to have taken control of the situation after he and Muleskin had returned from the visit to Quitman. He could begin to see why she had gained her sobriquet of Double-Cinch Annie.

By the time day had dawned and he had managed to eat some breakfast, Nation was feeling a lot better. Afterwards, he, Annie and Muleskin sat on the back veranda smoking, the dog lying at their feet. Nation doubted whether a mug of coffee had ever tasted so good. Muleskin and Annie seemed to be in a reflective mood.

'You should have seen Gunsight in the old days,' Muleskin said. 'You wouldn't believe it could be the same town. The place used to be jumpin'.'

'So what happened?' Nation asked.

'Of course there was the cholera epidemic,' Annie replied, 'but things recovered some after that. Nope, the main cause of the decline was the cattle industry movin' on. The range round Gunsight was never ideal. You've seen yourself how rough some of the country is: blackjack thicket, mesquite, chaparral. Once they opened up the rich grasslands round Powder Valley and the Bighorn Basin, it spelled the end. Now they've moved on to Montana. Maybe we should have moved on too. I guess I kind of hoped things would change, that the town would pick up again.'

'You and Muleskin must go back aways,' Nation prompted.

'We sure do,' Muleskin replied.

'Muleskin was indispensable to me in those days,' Annie said. 'You could say he was my right-hand man. He helped run the place and keep order, especially if Marshal Quitman wasn't around for any reason.'

'That goddamn bear didn't help

things any,' Muleskin said bitterly, 'once he chewed my leg up.'

Annie reached out and placed her hand on his arm. 'There isn't any point in going over it all again.'

'Muleskin's got my sympathy,' Nation responded. 'I ain't exactly on good terms with the varmint myself.'

'Some day!' Muleskin muttered beneath his breath.

'That's enough about the past,' Annie said. She turned to Nation. 'Muleskin has told me somethin' of your story but it might be an idea if I was to hear it in your own words. I assure you it's not because I'm curious. It's just that if I have the facts clear, I might be in a better position to help.'

Nation felt comfortable with Annie and Muleskin and it didn't take him long to recount his story. When he had finished, Annie sat in silence for a time while they drank the coffee and built themselves fresh smokes. Eventually she spoke.

'You think that what happened to

Cliff and Henrietta may not have been an accident?'

'Yes. And the fact that someone took those shots at me would seem to suggest I'm right to think that way.'

'But who would know you're here in Gunsight?' Nation had no answer and could only reply with a shrug.

'What about this man, Duane Gunter,' Annie said. 'I can remember him. He still comes back from time to time. He used to help out on the Forty-Five. Maybe it's significant that he left the area shortly after Cliff and Henrietta were killed.'

'Didn't he have somethin' to do with Mrs Winslow at the grocery store?' Muleskin said.

His question remained unanswered. Nation was musing on Annie's words. 'Maybe Gunter was involved in what happened to Cliff and Henrietta,' he said, 'especially if it wasn't an accident.'

'Whatever the truth of the matter, the old Forty-Five place has been allowed to go to the dogs since then,' Muleskin remarked. 'It certainly ain't much of a prospect.'

'Oh, I don't know,' Annie replied. 'I reckon it could be made profitable if someone was to give it time and attention.'

'You said yourself the cattle industry is dead now in these parts.'

'Which isn't to say it couldn't be revived,' Annie replied, looking at Nation as she did so.

'I ain't ever had much hankerin' to take up ranchin',' he said. 'Besides, like you were just sayin', this wouldn't be the place to do it.'

'Some folks seem to have made a success of it,' Annie said. 'Take Selby Rackham at the Grab All.'

'The Grab All?' Nation queried.

'Yes,' Annie said. 'It's a big spread over by the Little Purgatory river.'

'You know Rackham?'

'Not personally. He used to work right here on the Forty-Five,' she replied. 'You remember him, don't you, Muleskin?'

'I remember him. I never took to the fella much.'

'Not many people did,' Annie replied. 'I don't know why. He did well enough by Cliff and Henrietta.'

'What happened to him after Cliff and Henrietta died?' Nation said.

'As far as I know, he took responsibility for selling the cattle. Then he moved on. There's nothing unusual about that. A lot of cowhands live that way, moving from range to range.'

'Well, it seems he did pretty well out of it,' Nation commented. Muleskin and Annie exchanged glances. 'I ain't implyin' anythin',' Nation continued. 'I'm just tryin' to get the picture straight. If Cliff and Henrietta's accident weren't an accident after all, it would be useful to know who might have been involved. You mentioned Duane Gunter. Now it seems there was someone else around at the time, this man Selby Rackham — who apparently runs a big spread of his own. You said it was near a river?'

'The Little Purgatory.'

'How far is that?'

'I don't know exactly,' Annie said. 'Not too far. Why?'

'You don't intend headin' over to the Little Purgatory?' Muleskin said.

'In view of what you told me, I'm figurin' to do just that. See if anybody can tell me more about this hombre Rackham. I figure it wouldn't do any harm to check him out.'

'Be careful,' Annie said. 'If someone's gunning for you, you'd better be on the alert all the way.' Her words seemed to silence them for a while. Finally Annie turned from one to the other of her two companions. 'If you've got no objections,' she said, 'me and Muleskin would sure like to go along with you.'

'It could be a wild goose chase,' Nation responded.

'That doesn't make any difference,' Annie replied. 'This goddamn town has been getting us both down. It would be a relief to leave Gunsight behind for a while.'

'Neither of us would miss the place even if we never saw it again,' Muleskin said. 'There's only one thing I got to ask.'

'Yeah? What's that?'

'Old Midway comes along too.'

Just at that point, Nation felt the dog's tongue on the back of his hand and leaned over to stroke its head.

'What do you think, Midway?' he said. The dog looked up at him through baleful eyes.

'I reckon he'd have somethin' sensible to say if only he could talk,' Annie said.

Nation thought for a moment, looking at the old-timer's face, and then he grinned. 'OK,' he said. 'I guess I oughta know there's no way we could leave Midway behind.'

3

Selby Rackham rode his horse up to the crest of a low hill and looked down on the range spread before him. It presented a huge panorama of rolling grassland, low hills and grazing cattle. At a considerable distance, he could see the sunlight glinting on the waters of the Little Purgatory River. It was strange to think that, not too long before, the entire region had been Indian country. Now it was all his. And he had started with nothing, hiring himself out to two-bit ranches like the Forty-Five till he had seen the light. It was a fool's game, riding the range in order to put money into another man's pocket. The Forty-Five had been just the start. Once you took the first step, it was easy: things seemed to follow one after another. From that point he had steadily built up his wealth and power till he now owned just about the biggest spread in southern Wyoming. And the Grab All was not the final destination. He would soon be in a position to realize a long-standing project, which was to buy himself an even bigger and potentially more lucrative spread in Montana. He had investigated the potential of ranching in the mountain valleys of the Rockies even before riding for the Forty-Five. There had been not a cloud on the horizon till now.

He watched as a figure detached itself from the surroundings and his foreman came riding up the slope. 'Well?' he rapped as Gunter stopped alongside him. 'Did you deal with Nation?'

Gunter looked uncomfortable. He shook his head. 'I think I might have hit him,' he said, prevaricating.

'Think? Might have? What sort of language is that?'

'I followed him to the cemetery. It was dark so I figured it was a good time. He must have ducked just as I opened fire. There was a dog. I can't be sure but . . . '

'But nothing!' Rackham yelled. 'I don't want to hear about no dog or anythin' else. I told you to remove this Nation varmint and it seems like you've messed up. I don't even know what you're doin' back here.'

'Maybe my aunt got it wrong,' Gunter began. 'Maybe Nation has nothin' to do with Cliff and Henrietta. Even if he has, it don't have to mean anythin'.'

In an instant Rackham's six-gun was in his hand and pointing at his foreman.

'Shut up! I'm not listenin' to any more excuses. You've got your orders. So go and carry 'em out and don't come back until you have. I don't want Nation anywhere near the Grab All. I want him dead. Hell, it ain't askin' too much. You can even take a few of the boys if you want. Only make sure you don't let me down again. Now get goin'!'

Gunter didn't wait for any second invitation. Digging his spurs sharply into his horse's flanks, he rode off.

58

There was a sneer of contempt on Rackham's face. For a moment he was tempted to put a bullet into his foreman's back but instead he placed the gun back in its holster. He had meant what he said. There would be no more chances for Gunter.

* * *

It was an oddly assorted party of riders that set out from Gunsight. Nation was riding his blue roan, Annie a rangy buckskin. Muleskin took the dapple grey, having made arrangements for the mule to be looked after in his absence.

'I figure I might need a hand up,' he said as he made some final adjustments to the horse's harness. He turned away and went through the batwing doors. When he appeared a few moments later, he was dragging a contraption behind him.

'Made it myself,' he said. 'It's a travois for Midway. He can ride with me in one of the saddle-bags, but I figured he might get a mite uncomfortable if he has far to go.'

'Not to mention the horse,' Annie said, bursting into laughter.

'I don't know what you're sniggerin' at,' Muleskin said. 'I trailed some heavy loads this way in my time.'

'I've seen a dog doin' the pullin',' Nation remarked, 'but I never seen a dog as the passenger.'

The travois consisted of two crossed poles which Muleskin proceeded to fasten to the shoulders of the grey. The free ends trailed behind and across them he had spread some blankets.

'Up you go, old fella,' he said. Midway ambled onto the blankets and after sniffing them carefully, lay down and put his head on his paws before looking up at the old-timer through a bloodshot eye.

'He's taken to it right away,' Muleskin said. 'I knew he would.'

'OK,' Nation said. 'If everyone's ready, let's get started.'

Riding at a slow but steady pace, they soon left the town behind them. Nation was not sad to see the back of it. Gunsight was an oppressive place; it felt good to be on the move. As they rode, Nation was occupied with the question of who could have known his identity or that he was in Gunsight — and he was finding it hard to avoid the logical conclusion. The only person who knew was Muleskin. He liked the old-timer and he owed him a lot. It didn't seem right to suspect him and he fought hard against it. He tried to put the matter from his mind and give his attention to the present moment.

★   ★   ★

Ma Winslow was sweeping the board-walk outside the grocery store when she looked up to see a group of five riders approaching. The few people who were out and about paused to look at them apprehensively and she felt a quiver of alarm herself till she saw that the leading figure was her nephew. She had not expected to see him so soon. It was only very recently that he had been in Gunsight. If she was expecting him to call on her, she was mistaken. The group of riders rode straight past and pulled up instead outside the old Broken Wheel saloon. They jumped down from their horses and, drawing their guns, burst through the batwing doors. They paused for a moment to look around.

'Hobbs, Mangold, take the stairs!' Gunter rapped. 'You two, come with me.'

He led the way into Muleskin's room and from there to the stable and the corral. One of the men he had sent upstairs appeared at a window.

'There ain't nobody up here!' he shouted.

Gunter was exasperated and smashed his fist against a veranda rail. 'We musta just missed him,' he said.

'Your aunt coulda been wrong about Nation bein' here?' one of his companions suggested.

Gunter turned on him with a glowering look of rage across his countenance. 'She's not wrong!' he shouted.

'Perhaps . . . '

'Shut up and let me think for a moment!' Gunter yelled.

He sat down on the veranda step, his head in his hands. After a few moments he jumped to his feet again. 'He can't have gone far,' he muttered.

He was struggling to make sense of the situation. He knew that the old-timer Muleskin lived here and that the place still belonged to Double-Cinch Annie. So where were they? Were they with Nation? It was odd that none of them were about. All in all, it seemed likely that they had all left together. He crashed his fist against the stanchion and then, in a blaze of anger, ran back into the house and began to smash up what few items of furniture he could find. The others grinned at one another. They had seen this sort of thing before. They watched as he clattered up the stairs and began to vent his rage on whatever was up there. The sounds of breaking furniture and the tinkling of glass resounded through the building but it wasn't long before his first fury had abated. He came thumping down the stairs.

'I figure they ain't been gone long,' he said. 'We'll soon pick up their trail.' The others lingered, irresolute. 'Come on, then,' he yelled. 'What in hell are you standin' there for? Let's go get 'em!'

Without waiting any longer, he turned and stormed out of the saloon, quickly followed by the others. Without so much as a glance around him, he stepped into leather and jabbed his spurs into his horse's flanks. In a cloud of dust, they rode out of town.

★ ★ ★

Buck Nation was in no particular hurry to reach the Little Purgatory river; he and his companions made their way slowly, not taking risks with any of their horses. As evening began to descend he called a halt and they made camp alongside a shallow stream in the shade of some cottonwoods. The air was chilly; after they had eaten they sat by the flickering flames of the fire with mugs of coffee in their hands and looked up at a sky filled with stars. A gathering breeze whispered in the branches and the stream lapped against its shallow banks. Lying alongside Muleskin, the dog began to snore.

'That old fella seems to spend most of his time asleep,' Nation remarked. 'He was snorin' like that the first day I rode into town.'

As he spoke the words something flitted across his memory. He was in the grocery store, looking through the window at Muleskin and his hound, both apparently dozing. Suddenly he realized that someone else apart from Muleskin did know about his arrival in Gunsight: Mrs Winslow, the woman in the grocery store. He had even told her his name. And now another memory flickered, something someone had said almost in passing about there being a connection between Gunter and the Winslow woman. He sat up, looking across the flickering shadows at his two companions.

'This might sound like a strange question,' he said, 'but what do you know about the woman who runs the grocery store?'

'Mrs Winslow?' Annie said.

'Yeah. What kind of a woman is she? Does she have any family? Did she know Cliff and Henrietta Nation?'

'No more than the rest of us,' Annie said. 'Cliff and Henrietta used to drop by for supplies from time to time when they were in town. As far as I know, she hasn't got any children. She was a widow woman — ' Suddenly she stopped.

'What is it?' Nation said.

Annie turned to Muleskin. 'Duane Gunter,' she said. 'Didn't he stay with her for a time when he first came to Gunsight?'

'Dang me, you're right,' Muleskin

said. 'I believe there was some sort of relationship between them.'

Nation remembered that Muleskin himself had once previously referred to the connection. Annie turned to him with an expectant look on her face.

'So why is it relevant now?'

'It might not be relevant at all, but on the other hand . . . ' He stopped, gathering his thoughts. 'We have two names: Rackham and Gunter, both of whom were associated with the Forty-Five and with what happened to Cliff and Henrietta Nation. Now, I couldn't figure out how anyone knew who I was or that I was in Gunsight. The only person who knew both those things was Mrs Winslow.' He turned to Muleskin. 'Do you remember, when I came into town I spoke to you and asked where I might get some supplies? You directed me to her.'

'Yeah, that's right,' the old-timer replied. 'I think I see now what you're drivin' at.'

'Maybe it's just a coincidence that

there's a link between Mrs Winslow and Duane Gunter, but you got to admit it's a mighty odd one.'

Annie considered his words for a few moments. 'If you're right,' she said, 'it means that either Mrs Winslow passed the information on to Duane Gunter or she took a shot at you herself.'

'Yeah, but I don't think it's very likely to have been Mrs Winslow. Besides, I caught a glimpse of whoever it was and it didn't look like any old woman.'

'So you're sayin' it must have been Gunter?' Muleskin said. 'Hell, that throws a whole new light on things.'

'It means we're on the right track,' Annie said. 'If it was Gunter who fired that shot, he must have something to hide. And it must be something pretty important if he was prepared to kill for it.'

'Somethin' to do with keepin' the truth about what happened to Cliff and Henrietta from comin' out,' Nation said.

Annie turned her head and looked

out beyond the firelight into the darkness. 'If he was prepared to kill once, he'll be ready to try it again,' she said.

Nation felt an urge to calm her fears. 'Don't worry. We're better off now than we were before,' he said. 'It's a big advantage to know your enemy.'

He was surprised to see a smile steal across her features. 'I wasn't worried,' she replied, 'just establishing the facts. Seems to me like we might need to set a guard. I'm volunteering for the first shift.'

Nation made to disagree but she was not to be moved. Consequently she took her station a little way from the fire while the other two turned in to grab some sleep. It wasn't long before the old-timer's snores were competing with those of his dog but Nation remained wakeful. Eventually he got to his feet and, being careful not to alarm her, made his way to where Annie was sitting.

'It isn't time yet for you to take over,' she remarked.

'I couldn't sleep,' he said.

'I've been thinking,' she replied, 'about what we were talking about earlier.'

'And have you arrived at any conclusions?'

'As a matter of fact, I have. Duane Gunter worked for the Forty-Five. But so did Rackham. If they were working together in those days, maybe they still are. What if Gunter is now workin' for the Grab All?'

Nation considered her suggestion before replying. 'It would make sense,' he said. 'If so, it's goin' to make the situation even more dangerous. I'd understand if you wanted to call it a day and go back to Gunsight.'

Annie put her hand on his arm. 'Muleskin and I came into this with our eyes open. We ain't gonna walk away from it.'

'Are you sure you speak for him?' he said.

'Muleskin and I are old friends. We think the same. We're with you all the way.'

Nation turned to Annie. She was

close to him and he became aware of her physical presence. He felt an urge to take her in his arms but, with a struggle, he resisted.

'Thanks, I appreciate it,' he mumbled. 'Look, why don't you go back and get some rest? I can't sleep. I would only be lyin' awake anyway.'

She hesitated, as if about to remonstrate with him, but instead she only nodded before rising to her feet. 'Goodnight,' she said. 'Take care.'

He watched her retreating figure as it passed in front of the dying embers of the fire. He felt disturbed and angry with himself but he didn't know why. What else could he have said or done? He was more awake than ever. Resting his back against a rock, he made himself as comfortable as he could and prepared for a long, hard night.

*　*　*

Doc Hurley came out of his office and began to stroll towards the centre of town. As he approached the livery stables he heard the sound of hammering. He stopped at the open doorway and peered inside. Tom Irwin, the handyman, was doing some repairs to one of the stalls.

'Hello, Tom,' the doctor said. 'You're just the man I want to see.'

'You got a job for me, Doc?' Irwin asked. 'Things have been kinda slack recently.'

'Is that why you dug that fresh grave?' the doctor replied.

'Sure. I don't like to wait around doin' nothin'. After all, it ain't likely to stay empty for too long.'

The doctor smiled. 'I guess that's guaranteed,' he replied.

'How did you know?' Irwin asked. 'I ain't spoken to you about it yet.'

'Someone told me.'

'Would that be the fella who's been stayin' over at the old Broken Wheel saloon?'

'Word gets around,' the doctor replied.

'I saw him ridin' out with Annie and Muleskin. I thought that was kinda strange. Old Muleskin don't get around much and I ain't seen Annie in a long time. But the really odd thing was that a gang of riders turned up there later.'

The doctor stroked his chin. 'Did you recognize any of 'em?'

Irwin shook his head. 'They didn't stay long and when they left they didn't look too happy.'

'This town could do with a regular marshal,' the doctor said. 'Maybe I'd better get over to the Broken Wheel and take a look.'

Leaving the handyman to carry on with his work, he set off down the road. It only took a few minutes for him to reach the old saloon. The batwing doors were open as usual and he wandered inside. His first glance told him everything he needed to know. The place was a shambles. The door to Muleskin's room stood open and he glanced inside. What little furniture there was had been completely destroyed. He hesitated at the foot of the stairs. Annie's rooms were private. Anyway, he knew what he would find. He pondered over what he had seen for a few moments and then made his way back to his house. He kept his horse in a field behind it; in a short space of time he was in the saddle and riding out to pay a visit on ex-marshal Quitman.

★   ★   ★

Night-time drew towards dawn and Nation remained watchful. He wasn't expecting any trouble and had just about decided to roll himself a cigarette when one of the horses began to stamp and snort. He got to his feet, drawing his six-gun as he did so. Silently, being careful not to wake the others, he quickly made his way towards the animals. They were standing with their ears pricked, sniffing at the air. Something was disturbing them. He listened for any tell-tale sounds but there was only the familiar rippling of the water and the sighing of the wind. He remembered his encounter with the bear. Suddenly he was startled by the sound of snarling and spun round, but it was only Midway. In another moment, the figure of Muleskin appeared.

'What is it?' he whispered.

'The horses are restless. I figure there's somethin' out there.'

The dog continued to snarl and made to move forward. Muleskin held it back. 'Midway figures the same,' he said.

'Let's take a look,' Nation replied. 'Hold on to the dog. He'll show us the way.'

They crept forward. The sky was clear and dawn was approaching. There was enough light for them to pick their way through the undergrowth. At a little distance the brush grew thicker. They came upon the stream again where cottonwoods and willows grew together with other timber. The dog had ceased snarling and seemed to have lost any scent.

'He woulda kept at it a few years

ago,' Muleskin whispered.

'Maybe we were wrong,' Nation replied. 'Maybe it was nothin' but a snake or a water rat.'

'We ain't doin' no good here,' Muleskin said. 'We may as well go back.'

They began to retrace their steps. Nation felt increasingly anxious and when he reached the camp his senses told him that something was not quite right. The dog began to sniff and scratch at Annie's blanket. Nation rushed over and knelt down.

'Annie!' he breathed. There was no reply. He tugged at the blanket and discovered that there was no one underneath. The bed was empty. Annie was gone.

'How could we have been so stupid!' he exclaimed. He looked at Muleskin with a look of anguish in his eyes.

'Maybe she ain't far! Maybe she decided to take a walk, get some water,' Muleskin replied.

Although they knew it was hopeless, they rushed to the stream and began to search up and down the banks. As the first rays of light climbed the sky, they returned to the camp-ground.

'We got ourselves to blame,' Nation said. 'We acted like a pair of greenhorns.'

There was no need for Muleskin to respond. Nation was right. They should never have left the camp.

'Duane Gunter!' Nation rapped. 'He must have tracked us. He probably intended to sneak up and kill us but settled for somethin' else once he realized we'd been alerted.'

'We don't know that for sure.'

'Who else could it have been? It was Gunter or some of his henchmen.'

'At least it seems Annie's still alive. They couldn't have shot her.'

'And give themselves away? No. At least we should be able to find some sign.'

Without wasting any time, they began to search for traces of the intruders. It wasn't long till Muleskin found what they were looking for: some footprints embedded in the mud of the riverbank. 'And look here,' he said. 'A piece of the riverbank has come away.'

'Could just have been the water,' Nation replied.

'No. The water's too low. And it's been displaced by somethin' from above rather than beneath.' He splashed his way across the stream. 'Over here there's part of another footprint.' He bent down to look closer. 'There are some more, but they're faint. I don't know how many of 'em there were, but it looks like they crossed the stream and then took advantage of the cover.'

'Not the direction we were lookin' in,' Nation said.

'I wouldn't expect Midway to get it wrong,' Muleskin replied, 'even if he is growin' old. There were probably more of the varmints over that way.'

'We didn't hear any horses,' Nation said.

'They must have left them further off and come at us on foot.'

Mention of the dog's name made

them pause. Nation looked down at Midway, who had followed them to the stream. 'What do we do with him?' he said.

'Guess we're gonna have to leave that travellin' contraption behind,' Muleskin said. 'He's gonna find it a mite uncomfortable, but he can ride in my saddle-bag. It's big enough. He's done it before.'

'We don't want to lose any time.'

'We won't. Just carry on as normal. He'll be fine.' He bent down and stroked the dog's head. 'You don't mind, do you, boy?'

The dog shook itself and water sprayed on their legs. 'There you go,' Muleskin said. 'There's your answer.' Without more ado he picked the dog up and dropped it into his saddle-bag. 'He's ready to go,' he said.

They mounted up and splashed across the shallow stream. The sun had risen and a thin mist rose from the ground. They rode a little further and then Muleskin pointed to something a little way to their right.

'Horse droppings,' he said. When they reached the spot, the trail left by the kidnappers was apparent even to Nation's relatively unpractised eye.

'They won't get away,' he hissed. 'We must be right behind them.'

Muleskin nodded but added a word of warning. 'They won't be stupid enough to imagine we won't follow 'em. They could be leadin' us straight into a trap. I want to find Annie just as much as you, but we'll need to be watchful. We won't do Annie any good by bein' careless and gettin' ourselves shot.'

Nation's expression was grim. 'We're wastin' time,' he said. 'Let's ride.'

* * *

Annie had been rudely awakened but though she struggled with her attackers, there was nothing she could do. She was no match against the two men who held her in a vice-like grip. She was

80

half-led and half-dragged across the narrow stream and through the bushes beyond. In a grove of trees at a little distance some horses were tethered and she was hoisted across the back of one of them. One of her captors mounted up behind her and they set off into the darkness. The movement of the horse jolted her at every stride and she felt the indignity as well as the discomfort of her position. It didn't last for long because presently the horse came to a halt and she was lifted down. There were two other riders but she could not make out their features very distinctly because of the darkness.

'You won't get away with this!' she managed to say.

'Shut your trap,' one of them said.

'I don't know — ' she started to say, just as she was hit across the mouth.

'I said shut up.' The man's hand went to his gun and he waved it in front of her face. 'One more word and I'll kill you.'

'Put that gun away,' another man

ordered. 'One shot and you'll have let Nation know just where we are.'

The gunman gave him an ugly stare. 'One of these days, Usher, you'll go too far,' he hissed. 'Who do you think you are, anyway?'

'Just do it, Denton,' the man replied.

The gunman hesitated for an instant and then slowly replaced his gun in its holster. 'What are we waitin' for, anyway?' he asked.

'Isn't that obvious? We're waitin' for the others, like we arranged.'

Denton spat and then turned away. For a few moments there was silence and Annie considered desperately whether there was any chance of making a break when they heard the sound of approaching horses.

'That's Gunter and Wilson now,' one of the men said.

Out of the darkness two riders emerged. 'Did you get the lady?' one of them snapped.

'Sure, we got her,' Denton replied. 'She's right here.'

Annie was peering closely at the new-comers. Although she had rarely seen Gunter since his departure from Gunsight, she thought she recognized the speaker.

'Good,' he said. 'At least that's somethin'. We can use her to flush out that Nation varmint.'

'That ain't all we can use her for,' Denton muttered.

'It won't take long till Nation realizes what's happened,' Gunter continued. 'We've done enough for tonight. Let's get out of here.'

'Why not go back and kill him and that old-timer right now?' one of the men remarked.

'Because he's been warned now,' Gunter replied. 'It might not be as easy as you seem to think.'

Usher regarded him with a puzzled look. He was unhappy about taking the woman. Was it necessary? However, there was no further dissent. Annie was lifted up onto one of the pack horses and, at a word from Gunter, they set off.

4

Selby Rackham had been thinking hard since Gunter had left. Assuming Gunter was successful this time in eliminating Nation, it would still leave him in a vulnerable position. What was to stop Gunter from blabbing at some point? OK, he had things to hide too — in particular his part in the murder of Cliff and Henrietta Nation. But would that be enough to make him keep quiet? He had been prepared to put up with Gunter so far; he had ensured his silence by taking him on and even promoting him to foreman on the Grab All. It was a nominal position. Most of the hard work was done by his trail boss, Schultz. But Schultz was beginning to show signs of resentment at his role. He had seen through the arrangement.

The situation, as it now presented itself, offered an ideal opportunity to get rid of both Nation and Gunter and appease Schultz — all at the same time. If there was one thing which gratified Rackham it was a plan which answered several requirements at once. Having reached a decision, he resolved to waste no time in putting it in motion.

He had just seen Schultz ride in, so he made his way to the stables. Schultz, removing his saddle, turned round at Rackham's arrival. 'Boss,' he said in acknowledgement.

'Everythin' OK down on the south range?' Rackham replied.

'Sure. Some of the fencin' needed repair.'

'Good man.'

There was a pause. Schultz wasn't sure what Rackham wanted and Rackham was deciding what he should say. In the end, he decided to express himself directly and play on Schultz's resentment of Gunter.

'Schultz,' he said. 'How would you feel about takin' charge of this place?'

'How do you mean, boss?' Schultz replied.

'Just what I say. How would you like to be in sole charge of the Grab All?' Schultz looked confused. 'The thing is, I'm plannin' on goin' away for a while,' Rackham continued. 'I've got to look at a spread near a place called Hooker's Bluff up in Montana so I might be away some time. You've worked for me a long time. I need somebody to take care of the Grab All, someone I can trust.'

'What about Gunter?' Schultz managed to say.

'Right now Gunter is away carryin' out some business on my behalf. I don't know how long it'll take him. To be quite frank with you, Gunter has let me down recently. And he ain't popular with the men. You can tell me if I'm wrong, but they don't seem to have the respect for him that's needed to run a place like the Grab All.'

Schultz didn't say anything. He was still unsure how to take what his boss was telling him.

'If you're willin' to accept my offer, I'd be leavin' everything down to you while I'm away. I'll inform the men that you're in charge, but I don't even think that's necessary. I've watched you at work. The men respond to you. So how do you feel about it?'

Schultz stood for a moment, his mouth slightly open, considering Rackham's offer. It seemed too good to be true. For a long time he had been forced to watch Gunter's star rise while his own declined. Now he was being given the chance to reverse all that. To be put in charge of the Grab All ahead of Gunter was something he could not have anticipated. And if he understood Rackham correctly, there seemed to be an implication that Rackham would not object if Gunter was made redundant — whatever that might imply.

'Sure boss,' he said. 'You know you can rely on me. You go ahead and do whatever you need to do and I'll see that the Grab All is properly looked after. It'll be in safe hands. You won't need to worry none.'

'I know,' Rackham said. 'That's why I

decided to ask you. I can head north now without needin' to concern myself about anythin' else.'

Schultz would have liked to know more about Rackham's plans but decided not to push his luck. But who knew? If Rackham was extending the scope of his operations, the arrangement might become permanent. He permitted himself to ask when Rackham intended leaving.

'First thing tomorrow,' he replied. 'Now that I've talked about this with you, I don't need to delay any further.'

'Thanks, Mr Rackham,' Schultz said.

'It's me should be thankin' you,' Rackham replied. He slapped Schultz across the shoulders. 'I'll have a word with the boys this evening,' he said. 'Come on over afterwards and I'll fill you in with a few details.'

He turned and walked out of the stables. Schultz watched him with a quiet glow of satisfaction before picking up a blanket to wipe down his horse.

* * *

Nation and Muleskin rode hard with every expectation of catching up with Gunter. After all, they weren't far behind. At first, it was quite easy to follow their sign, but as the day passed and the trail took them towards the foothills, the ground became stonier with outcrops of rock so that they could no longer be sure that they were on the right track.

'Gunter ain't no fool,' the old-timer said. 'He's done a pretty good job of throwin' us off his trail.'

Nation rose in his stirrups and looked around. 'He probably knows the country pretty well. He could be aimin' to dry-gulch us. I don't like the idea of bein' caught somewhere in those hills, but we can't leave Annie in their clutches. I guess we gotta just throw caution to the wind and carry right on.'

Muleskin nodded. Midway, whose head had emerged from his saddle-bag, uttered a bark.

'Seems like he's agreein' with you,' the old-timer said.

'He probably figures we're crazy,' Nation commented.

'He'd be right,' Muleskin replied. Spurring their horses, they rode on.

* * *

Ex-marshal Quitman heard the sound of hoof-beats and, looking out the window, saw Doc Hurley ride into the yard of his house. He moved to the door as Hurley dismounted and tied his horse to the hitch-rail.

'Hello, Doc,' Quitman said. 'Seems like this old place is suddenly becomin' popular.'

The doctor smiled. 'Just taking up your invitation,' he said.

They went inside and Quitman poured two glasses of whiskey. 'It's good to see you,' he said, 'but I reckon this isn't just a social call.'

'You're very astute,' Hurley replied, 'and you're right.'

Briefly, he described what had happened at the Broken Wheel. When he had finished Quitman took a few moments to weigh up his words.

'Those boys must have been lookin' for Nation,' he said, 'and they weren't leavin' any callin' cards.'

'It looks like it's not only Nation that's in a heap of trouble, but Annie and Muleskin as well,' the doctor replied.

Quitman finished his drink and placed the glass on a low table. 'You know,' he said, 'I'm gettin' a mite concerned about you, Doc. One time, and it wasn't long ago, you seemed to have settled for a quiet life.'

'Annie and Muleskin are my friends,' the doctor replied.

'Sure they are. Mine too.' He paused for a moment. 'You think this is all tied up with what that fella Nation was sayin' about Cliff and Henrietta?'

'I figure it that way,' the doctor grinned.

Quitman rose to his feet and crossed the room to where a couple of six-guns were hanging on the wall. He took them down and strapped them round his waist.

'I never reckoned on usin' these again,' he said, 'but maybe I was too hasty.' He looked towards his visitor. With a smile on his face the doctor drew back his coat to reveal a six-shooter in the belt of his trousers.

'Seems like we're both comin' out of retirement,' Quitman said.

* * *

When Rackham left the Grab All, he took with him a select group of his henchmen, ostensibly ranch-hands, but all of them former gunmen who had served him well in the past. The main reason was that he didn't know exactly what to expect when he reached Montana. It was as well to be prepared for all eventualities. In accordance with that maxim, he sent another group of gunslicks to take care of Nation.

He didn't trust Gunter. Gunter had

shown incompetence and that was one thing he couldn't ignore. He realized he was leaving the Grab All a little short-handed, but the place more or less ran itself and he genuinely trusted Schultz to do a good job in his absence. The more he considered the whole matter, the more satisfactory his plans appeared. He watched with confidence as the group he'd selected to deal with Nation set off early the next morning. Then he himself departed for Montana.

★　★　★

When Quitman and the doc left Quitman's house, they had only a vague idea about which way to go, so their discovery of the discarded travois owed something to luck. At first neither of them could work out its use till they discovered unmistakable evidence in the undergrowth of the presence of a dog.

'There was a camp here and whoever set it up had a dog with 'em. That could only be Muleskin and Midway,' Quitman said.

'Yeah. And that means Annie and this Nation fella too,' Doc Hurley replied. 'But where are they now?'

'If we found them so easily, there's a good chance those varmints who ransacked Annie's house would do the same.'

'Maybe, but we ain't seen no evidence of a struggle. They must have moved on. With any luck, we should be able to pick up their sign.'

The former marshal scratched his chin. 'I still don't like it,' he said. 'There must be a reason why they left this contraption behind.'

'Maybe they were just findin' it too awkward,' the doctor replied.

'Maybe. Guess all we can do is keep goin'. At least we know we're on the right track and they can't be too far away. It would be a big help if we knew where they were headed for when they left town.'

'Yeah. But wherever it was, there's got to be a connection with those mangy coyotes who wrecked the old saloon.'

'Tom Irwin didn't recognize any of 'em?'

The doctor shook his head. 'I should maybe have tried to get more information from him,' he said. 'I didn't go into it in a lot of detail. Once he mentioned they'd been at the Broken Wheel, I just wanted to get over there and see for myself what they'd done.'

'You did right,' Quitman said. 'Come on, we'll find 'em.'

With a last glance around, they turned their horses towards the stream.

★　★　★

The trail which Nation and Muleskin were following was becoming steeper and stonier; sycamore and cottonwood trees looked pale and dusty in the sunlight. It was hard to follow the sign left by Gunter and his gang but Muleskin was able to detect traces of their passage where Nation would have had to admit defeat. It was clear to them both that they must have fallen a good way further behind their quarry than when they set off. As they progressed slowly, Nation's eyes searched the country, seeking for any place where Gunter and his men might be concealed. They each realized that they were taking big risks, but in a strange sort of way Nation would almost have welcomed an ambush. That way, at least, their enemies would be revealed. He was growing tired and was surprised at the old-timer's resilience. They had spent a long day in the saddle and the terrain was demanding. Suddenly the dog began to growl and then to bark.

'What is it?' Nation snapped.

'He's sensed somethin'. Probably just a skunk or a raccoon.' Muleskin brought his horse to a halt and looked around. 'Could even be a goddamn bear,' he added.

'The horses don't seem to be too bothered,' Nation replied.

They moved on and after a little distance they found raccoon tracks in the sand around a brackish pool near an outcrop of rock.

'That's probably what set him off,' Muleskin remarked.

Nation was thinking that the noise of the dog could have apprised Gunter of their presence. It didn't matter. He probably had them in his sights as it was. It might even be a good thing. If Gunter was nearby, then Annie would have heard and perhaps be encouraged, knowing they were not far behind. His thoughts were broken into by the voice of Muleskin.

'Used to have me a pet raccoon. Called him Clint. He were a good fella. The trick is to catch 'em when they're young.'

Whatever else the old-timer might have been going to say was cut off by a deafening burst of noise; Muleskin fell backwards from his horse while Nation's roan reared and threw him heavily to the floor. Nation realized instantly that they had been bushwhacked. Bullets were tearing up the dust and sand. Nearby, he saw a fallen sycamore log. Rolling over, he grabbed the old-timer by his jacket and hauled him to its shelter. The horses had bolted, taking their rifles and the dog with them, so he drew his six-guns and began to return fire blindly, aiming towards the rocks. He cursed out loud, conscious that he and Muleskin had been stupid not to have realized that the rocks offered the sort of cover Gunter and his men would be looking for. The din of gunfire quieted for a moment and he had a chance to look more closely at Muleskin, who had been stunned by the fall from the horse. At that moment his eyes opened.

'Am I still alive?' he muttered.

'You sure are, you old son of a gun.'

The old-timer glanced at his shoulder. 'It hurts,' he said, 'but at least it ain't my gun arm.' He sat up and, drawing his six-gun, turned to fire as a bullet slammed into the wood an inch from his head.

'Lie low!' Nation hissed.

Muleskin grinned. 'It ain't much in the way of cover,' he said. The next moment his gun spat flame and lead as Nation took the opportunity to jam more slugs into the chamber of his weapon. A fresh burst of firing from their ambushers sent shards of wood flying round their ears.

'We might be able to hold out here for a while,' Muleskin said, 'but sooner or later they're gonna get us.'

Nation's expression was grim. 'We'll see about that,' he replied.

His eyes roamed the scene for a possible way out, but nothing presented itself. They were lucky to have found the log where it was. All around it the terrain was bare. There were some trees and bushes at a little distance, but too far for them to have a realistic chance of making it to their cover without being killed in the process. At that moment a fresh wave of gunfire tore up the area around them.

'We can't do anythin' to change our position,' Nation yelled, 'but neither can they. If there was more cover, they might have been able to outflank us.'

For the moment it was an uneven stalemate. Nation wondered what had happened to the horses and raised his head. Instantly a shot rang out and bark flew into the air from the log. He ducked down instantly and lay back, looking up at the sky.

'If we can hang out till dark, we might be able to make a getaway,' he said.

Muleskin didn't like to disabuse his friend so said nothing, even though he considered their chances would be less than slim. It would be what the gunnies expected. 'At least we got plenty of ammunition,' he replied.

'Yeah, but I wish I had that rifle.'

'A field gun would be better,' the old-timer said.

Nation uttered a grim chuckle. 'Which side were you on in the war?' he remarked.

'The right side,' Muleskin replied.

The gunnies' fire had dwindled and there was comparative silence. Through it they became aware of another sound:

the drum of hoofbeats.

'If they're bringin' up reinforcements,' Muleskin said, 'I think we're done for.'

Nation strained his ears to listen. The hoofbeats seemed to be coming from their rear, but who else could it be other than more of Gunter's men? The sound grew louder and then suddenly a rifle-shot rang out. Nation turned to face the new danger, but as he did so a fresh burst of fire broke out from behind the rocks. At the same moment Nation caught his first glimpse of the newcomers. There were two riders and, just ahead of them, a dog. There was something vaguely familiar about them.

'Holy Moses,' Muleskin yelled, 'it's Quitman and the doc with old Midway!'

The newcomers were blazing away with their rifles as they rode but they were still out of range. As Nation watched them, he became aware of noise and movement in front of him, and presently Gunter and his men emerged briefly into view beyond the rocks; they had mounted their horses and were riding quickly away from the scene of action. At the same moment Midway leaped over the fallen log to land more or less in Muleskin's arms.

'Midway, old fella!' he shouted. 'You've come to the rescue!'

Quitman and the doc rode past them but quickly drew rein when they realized the opposition had melted away. A few shots rang out from the retreating gunnies but they presented no danger. Nation and Muleskin got to their feet as their rescuers dismounted.

'Hell, are we glad to see you!' the old-timer cried.

'I don't know what you're doin' here, but you couldn't have come at a better time,' Nation added.

The doctor's quick eyes saw that the old-timer had been hurt. 'Better get that shoulder attended to,' he said. 'You danged coyote. You're too old to be gettin' mixed up in this sort of thing.'

The old-timer's face was creased in a grin. 'It'll take more than a tumble from a horse to keep me out of the game,' he said.

Quitman turned to Nation and was about to say something when Nation stopped him. 'We can leave the explanations for now,' he said. 'Come with me. The varmints took Annie. Let's see if we can find anythin'.'

Together they ran forward to where the gunnies had been concealed. Nation was hoping against hope that Gunter might have left Annie behind but when they got to where the gunslicks had been concealed he was disappointed; there was no trace of her. They found something, however. One of the gunslicks lay dead in the dirt with a bullet in his chest. They didn't stop to examine the corpse but moved up the trail to where, a little way beyond, they found where Gunter and his men had left their horses.

'They skedaddled pretty quick when they saw us arrive,' Quitman said.

'It's one thing to bushwhack folk; it's another thing when the odds are more even. You can be sure that when Gunter realizes there are only two of you, he'll be back again.'

'Yeah, and maybe he'll have more numbers next time. But what about Annie? What happened? We found your camp; leastways we guessed it was yours when we found that old travois.'

'That was for Midway. Muleskin fixed it up.'

'You both owe that dog, one way and another,' the former marshal replied. 'We heard the shootin' just now but it was the dog made us realize which side was which.'

'Let's get back to Muleskin and the doc,' Nation said. 'I guess we all got some explainin' to do.'

* * *

The only reason Annie had not given Nation and Muleskin a warning was that Gunter had ordered her mouth to be gagged. She had been left in the care of one of the gunnies whose job was also to keep an eye on the horses. From her position she had heard the firing, but had no idea of the progress of the fight or of its outcome till Gunter and his boys had come running back to mount their horses and ride away. She noticed that there was one less of them. She had attempted to resist but it was to no avail. She took comfort from the fact that there had been a fire-fight at all. It could hardly have been part of Gunter's plans and could only mean that somehow Nation and Muleskin had survived the first blaze of fire. She had no way of knowing whether they were alive or dead, but from the way Gunter and his men behaved she was encouraged to believe that they might have survived.

They rode as hard as the terrain allowed, till eventually they pulled to a halt beneath a wall of rock. Glancing up, she saw the entrance to a cavern which showed as a blacker feature against the darkness of the night. It was obviously familiar to Gunter. She suspected that he had used it before. She remembered him from former days; it seemed he might have spent at least part of the time since then riding the high country, probably on the wrong side of the law.

'This is it,' Gunter said. 'We'll rest up here.'

They rode right into the mouth of the cavern, which was even bigger than it had first seemed. There was plenty of room for both men and horses. The overhang was high above their heads and Annie had no idea how far back it went. They built a fire in its depths, out of view of the trail they had ridden up, but the firelight made little impression on the gloom and only made the dark interior more mysterious.

'Take off her gag,' Gunter ordered.

It was a huge relief to her to be able to breathe more freely; but, as if to off-set the removal of the gag, the gunnies then tied her feet while leaving her arms free. Gunter leered at her and gave her his usual warning not to try anything.

As far as she could see, it was superfluous. There wasn't anything she could do. She was thankful that so far Gunter's men had confined their abuse of her to crude remarks and lascivious comments. For that she had to thank the softening influence of the man called Usher, who had stepped in a couple of times to admonish the others. How long it would remain that way was a different matter.

The night wore on. After having eaten, Gunter and his men remained by the fire, talking. Annie had not failed to notice the Grab All brand on their horses, but they were certainly not the ordinary run of cowboys. If Gunter was in the pay of Rackham, he wasn't the only one, and they were a rough bunch. As it grew late, the gunnies began to turn in for the night. She had been placed against one wall of the cavern, further back but just within range of the firelight. One foot was becoming numb; they had later bound her arms as well as her feet and the rope bit into her flesh. She wondered what they intended doing with her, and her conclusions were not reassuring. She assumed that Gunter was using her as a bait to draw in Nation. If he succeeded in killing Nation and Muleskin, she would have no further value. In any case, since she knew Gunter, it wasn't likely he would spare her.

Casting about for a means of escape, she began to search the rock wall of the cave with her knuckles for any sharp projection against which she could fray the rope. There was nothing; the walls of the cavern were smooth. She tried to work the ropes loose by moving her fingers and toes, but the ropes were too tight. Just as she was about to give up she became aware that someone was near her, and a voice whispered in her ear.

'Don't make a noise. I'm cuttin' you loose.'

She felt something sawing at the ropes that bound her wrists and then whoever held the knife slithered forward and began to work on her feet. In a few moments the ropes parted. The man's face came close and for the first time she could make out Usher's features.

'I don't agree with taking a lady,' he said. 'Follow me and don't make a sound.'

She rose unsteadily to her feet and stood for a moment to allow the circulation to resume as Usher signalled for her to follow him. She gritted her teeth but when she stepped forward she found that she was able to move quite freely. Carefully, she followed the dim shape ahead of her. He led her by the walls of the cavern, keeping in the shadows and avoiding the faint glow of the fire. Men were sleeping but she expected one of them to awake at any moment. Then she saw the dim looming shape of the cavern entrance. Where was the sentry? She could only follow the shadowy figure of Usher as he led her through the soaring cavern entrance and into the open air beyond. They were unchallenged; she realized that Usher himself must be the sentry on watch.

When they had passed a little way beyond the cavern, he stopped and she drew to a halt next to him.

'There's no time for explanations,' he whispered when he saw her about to speak. 'Like I said, I don't go along with kidnappin' ladies.' He pointed with his finger. 'There's a horse tied to a tree along there. Whatever you do, don't make any noise.'

'What will you do?' Annie said.

'Don't worry about me. I'll try to put them off the track with some kinda story. Just start ridin' and keep goin'.'

He pointed again and then, without further ado, he moved silently back towards the cavern. For a moment Annie hesitated and then she began to walk in the direction he had indicated.

She hadn't gone far when she saw the horse. She untied it and climbed into the saddle. Touching its sides gently with her feet, she guided it along the trail. Her heart was beating. What if something should happen to stop her now? The horse might make a noise. Usher might disturb one of the sleeping gunnies. When she had put a reasonable distance between herself and the cave, she urged the horse into a trot. She was tempted to go faster but she retained enough of her wits to realize that it would be taking a big risk in the darkness. She was a decent rider and it wasn't the first time she had ridden by night. As she drew further away from her captors, she began to think for the first time of all the other dangers which might present themselves and to wish fervently for the first signs of dawn.

*   *   *

When Nation and his three companions rode out the morning following the shootout, it didn't take them long to find the cavern. They approached it with caution, fearing another ambush, but it was deserted. Muleskin soon found evidence of it having been recently occupied.

111

'We must still be on the right track,' the doctor said.

'They'll be more careful next time,' Nation replied, 'now they know we got reinforcements. It sorta evens things up some.'

Muleskin stood by the entrance to the cavern, deep in thought. 'I figure there's a good chance Gunter will call it a day and head right back to the Grab All,' he concluded. They thought about it for a few moments.

'Maybe we should just make for the Grab All too,' Quitman said.

'What about Annie?' Muleskin replied.

Nation scratched his chin. 'They've got Annie with them,' he said. 'If we're right and we head for the Grab All, we won't be leavin' her behind.'

'We might be able to pick up Gunter's sign as we go,' Quitman remarked.

'Let's take a few more minutes to look around this place,' Nation concluded. 'If we don't find anythin' to change our minds, we'll set out for the Grab All.'

★ ★ ★

Selby Rackham and his hardened bunch of gunslicks made good progress on their ride north. The way was easy, and it wasn't till they were in the neighbourhood of the Black Hills that they were faced with a choice when the trail divided. Rackham, however, had done his homework.

'One route takes you to the Powder River Valley and the Big Horn Basin,' he said. 'The other one's for us; north to Montana.'

His words seemed to stir something in his listeners. One of them, in a burst of enthusiasm, threw his Stetson in the air and, drawing his six-gun, began to fire at it. Rackham grinned.

'Take it easy, Riff,' one of the men said. 'Some of those Sioux varmints might not have quit the reservation.'

'Just takin' a little practice,' the gunman replied. He jumped down from his horse and picked up the hat. There were two neat holes in it.

'Looks like you ain't lost your touch,' Rackham said.

The man laughed and, placing his foot on the stirrup, stepped back into leather.

'OK, boys,' Rackham shouted. 'Let's take the trail to Montana.'

They rode on, and as they did so Rackham was thinking that the joke about the Sioux might not be so wide of the mark. Even as far north as Montana, on the other side of the old Sioux country, they might still encounter scattered bands of hostile Indians. It was another reason he had brought his gang of gunslingers with him. It paid to be careful. That was why he had sent out enough men to make sure of killing Nation. He didn't know anything about him, but in view of past events at the old Forty-Five, the name was enough.

For a few moments his thoughts were on Gunter but they soon switched to other things. Gunter had failed him once. He had been warned, so he wasn't likely to fail a second time. And if he did, Rackham had put other men on the job.

★   ★   ★

When the first rays of dawn lightened the sky, Annie began to feel a little better. She carried on riding, following Usher's instructions and hoping to see some familiar landmark. As the sun climbed higher, however, she was forced to admit to herself that she was lost. She drew the horse to a halt and got down. She had eaten little the night before and was beginning to feel hungry. She felt in the saddle-bags and found some strips of jerky and a flask containing water. It wasn't much but she appreciated Usher's foresight in providing her with something. She sat down with her back against a tree and made the best she could of it. When she had finished she gave some water to the horse and then began to look around. She didn't recognize anything. She decided to ride further and try to reach some elevated point from which she could get a better view of the surrounding country.

Some time later she saw what she was looking for: a cluster of rocks. When she reached them she dismounted and began to clamber up. As she approached the summit, she saw a suitable foothold and stretched out a leg to reach it. Her skirt caught on her foot and she lost her balance, falling backwards onto the rock below. She landed awkwardly. Her leg was trapped beneath her and her foot hurt. She succeeded in disentangling her leg but when she made to sit up she gasped with pain and sank back again. She couldn't tell for sure, but she felt that she might have twisted her ankle.

She managed to prop her back against the rock so she could sit upright and take notice of her surroundings. A little way below her the horse had wandered away and was chewing some grass. She suddenly felt thirsty but she had put the flask of water back in the saddlebag.

She realized she must stay calm. What did they once call her? Double-Cinch Annie? Well, having got herself into an awkward situation, now more than ever she needed to stay in control.

* * *

When Gunter awoke to find that Annie was missing, he was furious. 'Who was on guard?' he yelled.

His men looked at each other with mildly concerned expressions on their faces. They had little respect for the foreman of the Grab All and his blustering did not have much effect on them.

'Someone's gonna pay!' Gunter fulminated.

'Instead of shouting about it,' Usher said, 'why don't we try and act sensible and see if we can find her. She can't have got far.'

Gunter turned to him. 'You'd better not have had anythin' to do with this,' he spluttered, searching for a scapegoat.

'Come on, boys,' Usher said. 'Let's

start lookin'.' He led the way out of the cave. The men, not knowing quite what to do, followed him when he turned in the opposite direction from that in which he had led Annie.

Gunter began to pace backwards and forwards in front of the cavern. He watched as the others carried out a search of the immediate vicinity but it was a while before he thought of the horses. He moved swiftly down the trail along which Usher had guided Annie; when he reached the horses he realized at once that one of them was missing. Cursing out loud, he spun round and ran back towards the cavern, shouting as he did so. 'One of the horses is missin'! She's taken one of the horses!' Although it was only a short distance, he pulled up outside the cavern, panting and breathless.

'What's that you say?' Usher asked.

'What's wrong with you?' Gunter shouted. 'Can't you understand? I took a look where we left the horses and one of them is gone.'

'Are you sure it ain't just broke loose?'

Gunter's hand dropped towards his six-gun in an instinctive gesture but he stayed his hand. He looked from one to the other of his men, trying to think. His first idea was to get on the woman's trail; but then Nation and his comrades were not far behind. Maybe they should stay and set another trap. Nation would see immediately that the cavern was a likely place for an ambush. Perhaps it would be better to find somewhere less obvious. He looked up at the sky. Dawn couldn't be far away. He needed to keep ahead of Nation. That was the priority. Once he had dealt with him there would be time to catch up with the woman and give her what she deserved.

'OK,' he said at last. 'Somehow, the woman's escaped. She won't get far. Right now we need to move on. Let's get out of here.'

As the men moved to follow Gunter's orders, Usher felt Denton's eyes on him. The man didn't like him. He carried a grudge. Did he suspect that he, Usher, was behind the woman's escape? Where Denton was concerned, it would be wise to watch his back.

5

Morning was well advanced when Schultz looked up from the fence he was mending to see four riders in the distance. They bore down on him at a steady pace; he walked back to where his horse was standing and took his old Henry rifle out of its scabbard. He observed them as they approached: one old-timer and the others pretty well on in years too. The riders drew to a halt.

'Howdy,' Nation said.

'Howdy,' Schultz replied. 'You boys goin' somewhere?'

'Is this the Grab All? We ain't seen no sign sayin' so since we left the Little Purgatory river.'

'This is the Grab All. Who's askin'?'

'The name's Nation. What's yours?'

'Schultz. I'm runnin' the spread.'

Nation paused, taking in the information. 'We're lookin' for a man called

Rackham. We were under the impression he owns the place.'

Schultz eyed them suspiciously, vaguely conscious that he might have given too much away already. Midway's head appeared from the old-timer's saddle-bag and he started. He didn't spend long speculating about the dog, however, because over Nation's shoulder he could see a group of Grab All men riding towards them with rifles in their hands.

'I don't know what you boys want,' he said, 'but I figure you'd best turn around and head back wherever you came from.'

'Don't get us wrong,' Nation said. 'We don't mean to cause any trouble.'

'Trouble is what you've found,' Schultz said. Nation heard the sound of the approaching horsemen and turned in his saddle. 'There are others where they came from,' Schultz said. 'I'm surprised you haven't run into any of 'em already.'

'We ran into Gunter,' Nation hazarded. 'He cut and run. In fact, we figured he might have got here ahead of us.' It was clear to Nation that Schultz was disconcerted at the mention of Gunter's name.

'Gunter,' he repeated unconvincingly. 'Who's Gunter?'

Nation glanced around him. The Grab All riders had come up and enclosed them in a half-circle. One of them spoke to Schultz. 'Is there a problem, boss?'

'No problem. These gentlemen were just about to leave us.'

Nation turned to face the newcomer. 'We ain't lookin' for trouble. We have a message for a man called Rackham. Folks tell us he runs a spread called the Grab All. Apparently this is the Grab All. So why not just take us to him?'

The man exchanged glances with Schultz but neither of them said anything. A tense silence seemed to have everyone in its grip till Schultz spoke again. 'Where is Gunter?' he said.

Nation grinned. 'I thought you didn't know the name,' he replied.

'Whether I do or not is no business of yours.'

'It is when he tries to bushwhack us.'

'Then your issue is with Gunter, not Rackham.'

Nation thought for a moment. The situation was a stalemate, but one in which Schultz and his men held the upper hand.

'You're right about us havin' an issue with Gunter,' he said. 'It's my belief he's headed this way. If you see him, tell him he'd better not have hurt Miss Annie.'

A puzzled look spread across Schultz's features. 'Miss Annie?' he queried.

'She's a friend of ours. Gunter took her captive. If he shows up here with Miss Annie in tow, I'd be obliged if you'd do somethin' to remedy the situation.'

Schultz's expression changed from one of puzzlement to distaste. He had reason to want Gunter to remain absent. He was enjoying being in charge of the Grab All and he didn't relish the prospect of Gunter upsetting the apple cart. He had more than a suspicion that Rackham had grown tired of having Gunter around.

And he didn't like the suggestion of a woman being mistreated. The situation was delicate and he wasn't sure about the best way to resolve it. He felt under pressure. He needed more time. It could do no harm to take the intruders back to the ranch-house.

'I don't know what this is about,' he said, 'but I intend to find out.' He turned to the man who seemed to be the spokesman for the rest of the Grab All hands. 'Keep your rifles ready,' he said. 'We'll take 'em back to the ranch and then decide what to do with 'em.'

He turned to his horse and vaulted into the saddle. 'You can see how things stand,' he said to Nation, indicating the surrounding men. 'If I were you, I wouldn't think of tryin' anythin'.'

Nation shrugged. 'Why would any of us do that? Like I said, we don't want any trouble.'

'In that case,' Schultz said, 'you won't have any objection to handing over your weapons.'

Nation quickly weighed up the

situation. He glanced at the others and Quitman nodded. 'OK,' he replied, 'just so long as we get 'em back again.'

Schultz signalled to a couple of the Grab All men; they jumped from their horses and collected the armaments. As one of them was removing Muleskin's rifle the dog snarled and the man jumped back. A few of the others laughed. It seemed to release some of the tension which still hung in the air.

'He bites as well,' Muleskin said. The man threw him a disgruntled look.

'OK,' Schultz said. 'The fun's over. Let's go.'

* * *

Gunter's intention had been to stay ahead of Nation and also to find the woman; but when he failed to discover any sign left by her horse, he decided that it might be a better idea to return to the Grab All. Rackham had indicated that he would be leaving the Grab All for a time in order to ride north to

Montana. With any luck, he might already be gone. He was mulling the matter over when they found the horse the woman had taken to make her escape. It meant that, quite by chance, they had located her; the horse couldn't have travelled far.

'What do you think happened?' Denton said.

'I don't know,' Gunter replied. He drew out his field glasses as Usher urged his horse forward.

'Want me to take a look around?' he said, trying to conceal his anxiety.

Gunter gave him a searching look. 'What's up with you, Usher?' he said. 'You got some kind of interest in the lady?'

Usher simulated a coarse laugh. 'Yeah, sure,' he replied. 'And I figure I ain't the only one.'

Gunter continued to stare at him. 'We'll all take a look around,' he said. 'And I figure we start with that mound of rocks over there.'

He returned the glasses to their case and set off, followed by the others.

There were clear indications that the horse had come from that direction. When they reached the rocks, the gunslicks slid from their horses and began to climb. They full expected to find Annie, so it came as a disappointment when they failed to do so.

'She's got to be round here someplace,' Gunter snapped. 'She must be hidin' close by. Spread out, men, and keep lookin'.'

They continued to search and were soon rewarded by a cry from Denton. 'Over here! I figure I've found somethin'.'

They rushed to join him and he pointed at the ground. There were faint marks on the stony surface which had been left by hoofs. Nearby they found horse droppings.

'What the hell is goin' on?' Gunter yelled.

Denton bent down and examined the sign more closely. 'I'd say there were a few horses,' he said. 'Take another look yourself.'

Gunter and the rest of the men did as Denton suggested. As they did so, Usher was thinking hard. At first he hadn't known whether to feel relief or alarm at not finding the woman hiding among the rocks, but now he was beginning to feel better because he had come up with the obvious explanation. Nation and his comrades must have found her, in which case she was in safe hands again. It took Gunter only a little more time to arrive at the same conclusion.

'It must be that Nation varmint,' he said. 'Who else could it be?' He swore and dashed his fist. When he had finished cursing he looked at the others.

'Well,' he said, 'it shouldn't be too hard to follow their tracks. We'll catch up with them soon enough. And when we do . . . ' He left his words unspoken but the others didn't need to be told.

* * *

Schultz had been doing some rapid thinking while he and his men escorted

Nation and his comrades back to the Grab All ranch-house. The upshot of it was that if Nation had an issue with Rackham, it was none of his concern. On the other hand, if he had an issue with Gunter, then the opposite was true and it might be to his advantage to side with the newcomer. It seemed that Gunter could not be far behind and the scene was being set for some kind of showdown.

'I find it hard to believe that Mr Rackham could have been involved with any skulduggery such as you suggest,' Schultz said when Nation had outlined the story of the former events which had taken place at the Forty-Five, 'but I got to admit I don't feel that way about Gunter.'

'You'd better make up your mind what you intend doin' about the situation,' Muleskin said, 'because he could be here any time.'

'I never figured Gunter would stoop so low as to kidnap and threaten a woman,' Schultz mused.

Just then they were interrupted by a knock on the door. It swung open and one of the ranch-hands entered.

'Thought you'd like to know, Mr Schultz,' he said. 'A big group of men are headed this way. Mort saw 'em through his field glasses.'

'Thanks. You did the right thing,' Schultz replied. 'Go over to the bunkhouse and warn the boys there could be trouble.'

The man nodded and made his exit. Schultz stood for a moment, undecided. Events were moving too fast for him and he was caught in a quandary.

'What'd I just say? I figure that must be Gunter,' Muleskin said.

Schultz was puzzled. 'How many men did you say he had with him?' he asked.

Nation shrugged. 'We figured not more than half a dozen.'

'Jud said there was a big bunch of 'em.'

'Maybe they rounded up a few more someplace.'

Schultz suddenly recalled the group of men who had ridden away from the Grab All the same day as Rackham. He had assumed they were part of Rackham's escort, but could he have been wrong? Maybe they had something to do with Gunter. He turned to Nation.

'Assumin' it is Gunter, why should I let it worry me?' he asked. Even to his own ears his words sounded hollow.

Nation got to his feet. 'Come on,' he said to the others. 'We've acquainted Mr Schultz with how things stand. After all, our business is with Rackham.'

They stood up and made for the door. Outside, some of the Grab All men levelled their rifles at them. 'Everythin' OK, Mr Schultz?' one of them shouted. 'Are you lettin' these folks go?' Schultz appeared in the doorway. His face was creased with anxiety and uncertainty.

'I tell you what,' Nation said, turning to him. 'If you've got no objections, we'll wait in the barn. Just in case we're needed.'

There was a lull. Muleskin gathered a gob of phlegm in his mouth and spat into the dust of the yard. 'I figure those riders must be gettin' mighty near,' he said.

Schultz stood irresolute. His men watched him closely, waiting for a word of command. Nation glanced at his comrades in turn; he thought he saw the shadow of a smile play over Muleskin's features. He heard the first sounds of galloping hoofs but he didn't have time to take in any further impressions because the air was suddenly rent by the sound of gunfire coming from somewhere beyond the yard.

'I think that answers your question about Gunter's intentions,' he snapped at Schultz.

There was more gunfire and Schultz's indecision came to an end. 'Take cover, everybody!' he shouted. Some of the Grab All men rushed past him into the ranch-house while others made for the barn. 'Your weapons are in the back room,' he said to Nation. 'Make sure you point 'em in the right direction.'

Nation grinned. 'You can count on that,' he said.

They rushed inside and Schultz slammed the door. Nation led the way into the back room where some of Schultz's men were already ensconced. 'Where do you want us?' he said.

Schultz had positioned his men at the windows where they could command a view of the yard.

'Come with me,' he replied, making for the stairs. As he did so he stumbled and almost fell. 'What the hell . . . ' he began.

'Midway!' Muleskin shouted. 'I was wonderin' what had become of you.'

The dog was jumping at him. Schultz gave them both a rueful look before continuing up the stairs. There was a landing and a short corridor with three rooms opening off it.

'Nation, you come with me,' Schultz shouted. 'Two of you take the big bedroom and the other the smaller one lookin' towards the back.'

All the while shooting had been continuing outside, although more sporadically following the initial outburst.

'What do you reckon is goin' on?' Schultz said to Nation as they took up position by the windows.

'I figure Gunter is a fool,' Nation replied. 'He had no cause to come in shootin' like that. He's played right into your hands.'

'It don't seem that way right now,' Schultz replied. 'He's got us pinned down and his men are professional gunfighters. Most of us can use a gun, but not like those *hombres*.'

'That was Rackham's way, was it?' Nation replied. 'To keep some gunslingers on hand just in case the ranch needed protection?'

Schultz didn't reply. He had worked with Rackham for a long time. The Grab All had provided for him; he had learned not to ask too many questions and he still felt a loyalty towards his old boss.

'You're right about Gunter having us

pinned down,' Nation continued. 'It ain't an ideal situation. I'm thinkin' that it might be a good idea for a few of us to break out while we still can.'

'Some of the boys made it to the barn and the bunkhouse,' Schultz commented.

'They're still not mobile. One or two out there with the freedom to move about could do a lot of damage.'

'I take it you got yourself in mind,' Schultz said.

Nation shrugged. 'That's up to you,' he replied.

'You'd better not be playin' any tricks.' Nation's eyes narrowed. 'OK, I take that back,' Schultz said. 'Good luck.'

Quickly, Nation dashed into the room where Muleskin and the doctor had taken up position. When he told them what he intended, Muleskin shook his head.

'I can't get along too well with this leg,' he said. 'Take the doc and I'll cover for him and Quitman.'

Nation could tell that the old-timer had spoken reluctantly but what he said made sense. 'OK,' he replied curtly. 'Let's get goin'.'

Gunfire had almost ceased for the moment, but Nation reasoned that simply meant Gunter's men were taking up their positions. In all likelihood Gunter had not anticipated any response to his initial outburst and was being more careful. There was no time for further delay. Signalling to the others to follow him, Nation made for the stairs and the back entrance to the ranch-house. Once outside, they paused for a moment but a sudden burst of fire and a spattering of bullets made them take to their heels. When they had reached the shelter of a corner of the barn they regrouped.

'What do you reckon?' Nation said.

Quitman thought quickly. 'Our horses are in the stable behind the corral,' he said. 'I figure we should get to 'em and then circle Gunter's gunnies. They won't be expectin' any attack from that direction.'

Nation turned to the doc. 'Seems like a good idea,' he said, 'if we can make it. Gunter's got men all around the place. Somebody's already spotted us. There's a good chance we'll run plumb into them.'

'The quicker we get on with it the better chance we'll have,' Nation said. 'Once we're safely behind 'em, we'll spread out. That way we might be able to convince them there are more of us. Come on, follow me.'

Quitman hesitated for a moment. 'What about Annie?' he said. 'How does she fit into the picture?'

Nation's jaw tightened. 'Try not to think about that,' he said. 'There's nothin' we can do except trust to luck and take the chance of gettin' to her if we can.'

Quitman nodded. His face was lined with pain and it suddenly occurred to Nation that maybe there had been something between the ex-marshal and Annie in the past. Could that be another reason why Quitman had elected to live so far out of town? The thought was brief; the need for action was urgent. Indicating for the others to follow him, he crouched low and began to run towards the corral behind which a stand of trees offered shelter.

Rifles cracked and bullets tore up dust uncomfortably close to their feet. They reached the corral and drew up for breath, crouched behind the gate. A slug tore into the fence nearby and shards of wood flew into the air.

'When I say go, go!' Nation snapped.

He gave the signal and they dashed forwards. As shots rang out they ran through the corral, vaulting the fence at the far end. The barn was just a little distance beyond and they reached it without mishap. Their horses were in the stalls, tossing their heads and stamping. Saddles hung from hooks in the wall. It took no time to harness the horses and lead them outside, where they stepped into leather and made for the shelter of the trees.

* * *

Annie could hardly believe her bad luck. She had escaped from Gunter only to fall into the hands of a second group of gunslicks who were now riding with him. They had left her tied to a tree while they all rode forward to cover the remaining distance between them and the Grab All. Since their departure, she had struggled to free herself, and now the sound of shooting inspired her to redouble her efforts. She had hoped the bark of the tree would be sufficiently rough to fray the ropes, but all she succeeded in doing was chafing and scraping her wrists till they were bloody with the friction. Even if she managed to free herself, she wasn't sure how far she would be able to walk. Her ankle felt better than when she first twisted it but she wasn't confident of being able to hobble very far. The ropes bit tight, but she continued struggling till she heard a rustling in the bushes. Fearfully, she glanced sideways and gave a gasp of surprise when she saw it was Muleskin's dog.

'Hello, fella,' she said. 'What on earth are you doing here?'

The dog whimpered and leaped up at her, licking her face. She moved her head and, despite her dire situation, managed to laugh. The dog was sniffing at her and then he barked and shuffled away into the bushes. She turned her head but couldn't see him. Moments later she felt something wet on her wrists and thought for a moment that they were bleeding afresh, when she heard sniffling and panting sounds and realized it was the dog.

'Good boy,' she said, a wild hope suddenly flaring up inside her. The dog was biting and worrying at the rope and she could feel it begin to fray. She tugged hard and suddenly the rope split. Her hands were free! Leaning forward, she started to undo the ropes tying her feet. The knots were tight and the task was difficult. She kept glancing about for any of the gunslicks but the sporadic sounds of gunfire a little way off assured her that they were fully occupied. But for how long? The dog was running about and jumping at her while she struggled with her bindings. Her fingernails clawed at the knots and broke with the effort but at last she had loosed them enough to be able to slip her feet free. With an effort she managed to pull herself up, supported by the trunk of the tree, as the last coils of rope fell away from her. The first thing she did was to bend down and stroke the dog.

'Good boy, Midway,' she said over again. 'What a good dog.'

She considered the matter. Should she try and get away from Gunter and his men, or should she seek the shelter of the trees and brush? She decided that to seek shelter was the best thing to do, even if it meant staying in the vicinity. She stamped the numbness from her feet and when she felt she was ready, moved back into the trees, followed by the dog.

* * *

Once they had put a little distance between themselves and the ranch-house, Nation and his two companions brought their horses to a halt.

'OK,' Nation said, 'so far, so good. Now the time's come to split up and try to get behind Gunter and his men. Take the position of the ranch-house as your guide.'

Quitman and the doc nodded. Turning their horses, they began to spread out. Behind them the sounds of fresh gunfire were stifled by the intervening woods. Ahead of Nation the trees thinned and he emerged into comparatively open country. He spurred his horse and rode hard, keeping his eyes open for any sign of the gunslicks. The sounds of battle now came from a different direction and he knew his plan of outflanking Gunter's men was working. He topped a short rise and had his first clear glimpse of what was taking place at the ranch-house. It was obvious where Gunter's men had taken up position. He only had to find cover within range of them to create a fresh angle of assault. Choosing a patch of brush, he dropped from the saddle, took his Winchester and opened fire. He could see immediately that his onslaught was effective. Shots were returned but it seemed the gunnies had only a vague idea as to where he was concealed. Presently he heard other shots coming from nearby and he knew that Quitman and the doc had joined in the struggle. He smiled grimly as he jammed more cartridges into the chamber of the rifle. His plan was clearly working and he was feeling confident of the outcome.

The volume of lead that was being flung in his direction had lessened and he decided to take up a position among the trees nearer to the ranch-house. He mounted his horse and moved down through the brush into the woods until eventually he slid from the saddle. He began to creep forwards. Suddenly he froze. Through the muffled sounds of gunfire he thought he had heard footsteps. He took position behind a tree and waited. He wasn't mistaken. Someone was close by, maybe more than one. Had they detected his presence? Perhaps they had found the horse. He peered through the undergrowth and caught a glimpse of something yellow. He was concentrating so hard that he didn't hear anything from his rear till the click of a rifle told him someone had the drop on him.

'Throw down the rifle!' a voice snapped.

He did as he was ordered. When he had done so he heard rapid footsteps behind him. Before he could turn, his arms were seized and he was held by two men in a vice-like grip. A third man approached him; his instinct told him that it was Gunter. When the man spoke he was proved correct.

'Unless I'm mistaken,' he said, 'I believe I've caught up with the elusive Mr Nation at last.' Nation's lips remained closed. 'Yes, I think I would recognize you even though I only caught a glimpse of you that night in Gunsmoke. You've proved to be quite a nuisance.'

He advanced and felt in Nation's pockets as if for confirmation. In a few moments his hand emerged with the attorney's letter. Quickly, he read it through.

'So you're now the owner of the Forty-Five,' he said. 'It's all beginnin' to fit into place.'

Nation did not attempt to deny his identity. He could see there was no point. He decided to confront Gunter directly.

'What happened to Cliff and Henrietta Nation?' he said.

Gunter's lip curled in an ugly leer.

'Haven't you heard?' he replied. 'They died in an unfortunate accident.'

'An accident? That's not the way I figure it.'

Gunter drew back his hand and hit Nation hard. 'So how do you figure it?' he snarled.

Nation's lip was split and blood trickled down his chin. Suddenly Gunter laughed.

'OK,' he said. 'I'll tell you how it happened. You're gonna die real soon anyway. It'll give me a lot of pleasure to enlighten you. You're right. It was no accident. I fixed that buggy to overturn and I made sure I was on hand to finish them off. Just in case. Oh, don't get me wrong. It wasn't my idea. I admit I wasn't clever enough for that. No, it was Rackham who thought it out, but I was more than happy to go along with it. Now he's got the Grab All. It's worked out fine for both of us.'

'That's what you think,' Nation replied. 'While you were out of the way lookin' for me, he put Schultz in charge.'

Gunter's leer was replaced by a look of fury. Drawing back his fist, this time he brought it crashing into the pit of Nation's stomach. He would have collapsed but for the men holding him up. For the briefest moment he thought of appealing to them but he knew it was useless. They were some of Gunter's chosen cronies. Through the pain and nausea he saw Gunter's gun-hand come up and he prepared himself for the bullet that would end his life. Gunter drew back the hammer. At the same moment, out of the corner of his eye, Nation saw a brownish form land on Gunter and cling to his arm. Gunter yelled, trying to shake it off. One of the men pinioning Nation relaxed his hold and in that instant Nation seized his chance.

Tearing himself free, he turned and smashed his fist into the gunnie's face. The man reeled backwards, and as he did so Nation ducked and drove at the other's stomach with his head. He felt the heavy impact as the man crumpled. Both men reached for their side-irons but, before either succeeded in drawing them, Nation's six-gun was in his hand and spitting lead. He heard barking and snarling sounds and realized that the brown object he had seen was Midway. A shot rang out and he gasped in pain as a bullet grazed his hand and the Colt fell to the floor. He looked up. Gunter had shaken off the dog and was standing with a grin on his face and his gun pointing at Nation's chest. Nation saw something else as well, and tried his best not to let his eyes give away the fact that standing just behind Gunter was Double-Cinch Annie. She held a tree branch in her hand and as Gunter became dimly aware of her presence she brought it crashing down on his head. He remained standing for a moment till a glazed look came into his eyes; he took one step forward and then toppled to the ground. For a moment Nation and Annie stood gazing at each other in disbelief till the spell broke and she ran forward to collapse in his arms. He held her tight, scarcely noticing the pain in his hand till she drew apart and took it in her own.

'You've been hit,' she exclaimed. He glanced down. His hand was a bloody mess. 'Here, let me bandage it,' she said.

When she had dressed the wound using a bandana, Nation checked on the men he had been forced to shoot. They were both dead. He turned to Gunter. He was unconscious but still breathing.

'My horse is just at the back of those trees,' he said to Annie. 'Can you fetch it while I see to Gunter?'

He swiftly tied Gunter's hands behind his back with his bandana and then, as the man began to come round, dragged him to his feet.

'OK, Gunter,' he ordered. 'Time we put a stop to this fightin'.'

Back at the ranch-house, the battle continued without either side gaining the upper hand. A couple of Schultz's men had been hit but so far nobody had died. They were putting up a brave show, but it wasn't their forte. Only Muleskin seemed to be positively enjoying it.

'Ain't had a scrap like this since the time the Cranford gang held up the Hollenberg stage and tried to take over the way-station,' he said. 'They were sure good times.' He looked about him. 'Say, you ain't seen Midway anywhere?' he asked. Schultz shook his head. 'I guess the old fella can take care of himself,' Muleskin added. 'He used to appreciate a good scrap too. Why — '

Further conversation came to an abrupt end as a bullet thudded into the shutter a couple of inches from his nose.

It was getting along in the afternoon when Schultz became aware that something new was happening. The shooting had been sporadic for some time but suddenly it had ceased altogether. A strange air of expectancy hung over the ranch. He looked out of the window frame but could see nothing. The men beside him wore somewhat puzzled expressions. Then he thought he heard the faint steady drum of hoof-beats. He returned to the window and peered out once more and this time he was rewarded by a strange and unexpected sight: a man with a rifle leading a horse on which another man was fastened by his wrists. It seemed to Schultz that the first man was taking a big risk but it didn't seem to bother him. The man on the horse, on the other hand, looked scared as he glanced anxiously about him.

Schultz's attention was riveted. He

stared more closely and then started back; the man on the horse was Gunter and the man leading it was Nation! He came to a halt outside the ranch-house.

'Listen, everybody!' he shouted. 'The show's over. If anyone tries anything, Gunter dies.'

Gunter's look expressed his terror. Nation muttered something to him and, in an unsteady voice, Gunter yelled:

'Do as he says!'

'Lay down your arms and come out of hidin'!' Nation ordered. 'This affair is finished!'

Schultz could hardly believe what he was seeing. After a short interlude a few of Gunter's gunslicks began to emerge. Others followed and some of his own men also started to come out from the barn and outhouses. He licked his lips and instinctively tightened his grip on the rifle. He was expecting trouble at any moment but nothing happened. The men started to acknowledge one another grudgingly. It was apparent that Gunter's gunnies had no real loyalty towards him. They seemed quite happy to call it a day. Taking his cue, he walked to the door and stepped outside. He stood on the veranda, looking down on Nation and his prisoner.

'Good to see you back again, Nation,' he said. 'Looks like you've won the day.'

'You and me between us,' Nation replied. He waved his gun for Gunter to get down from the horse, which he managed to do very awkwardly.

'You got somewhere we can put this varmint till he can be taken to the nearest jailhouse?' Nation asked.

Schultz's face broke into a wry grin. 'I reckon we can find someplace,' he said.

6

A few days had gone by. Nation was keen to move on to Montana but he realized that it made sense for them to lie up for a while. He and Annie needed some time to recover from their injuries. Her ankle wasn't as bad as she had at first feared and the doctor had done a good job on his hand. He had been fortunate; the bullet had torn along his palm without causing serious damage. All the same, it was his gun hand and he doubted that he would ever be so nimble on the draw again. The real hero of the hour was Midway and he was having the time of his life. For Schultz and his Grab All ranchhands, things had turned out well. However, Schultz was left with mixed feelings about Rackham. It was hard for him to realize that Rackham was not the man he had taken him to be, despite the evidence of having men like Gunter and Denton in his service.

On the evening of the day following the battle, they sat on the veranda of the ranch-house drinking coffee. The sun's disc hovered just above the horizon and a cool breeze had sprung up, shaking the leaves of the trees.

'Do you still intend goin' after Rackham?' Schultz said.

'That is our intention,' Nation replied.

Schultz took a mouthful of the steaming black liquid and swallowed hard. 'Well, I guess what happens between you and Rackham is none of my business,' he replied, but he didn't sound convinced. Nation sensed his mixed feelings.

'We ain't bounty hunters,' he said. 'If we ever catch up with Rackham, we'll do our best to bring him in alive. All we want is for him to face justice the same way as Gunter will.'

'Leave Gunter to me,' Schultz said. 'I'll take him to the marshal next time I'm in town.'

'Maybe we can catch up with Denton

too,' Annie said.

Annie had told them her story. It seemed that Denton and a few others had escaped following the fight and Nation had a feeling that they would be trying to reach Rackham. After she had spoken there was silence. Nation became aware that someone was approaching them. As he came near, Annie got to her feet and, despite the pain in her ankle, hobbled down the veranda steps to meet him.

'Usher,' she said. 'I hoped I'd see you. I haven't had a chance yet to thank you for what you did for me back there.'

The newcomer took off his hat in an awkward motion designed to hide his embarrassment. 'I'm glad you seem to be makin' a recovery,' he said.

'Come and join us,' Annie responded. She took his arm and drew him up the steps to the veranda.

'Howdy, Usher,' Schultz said. 'How are you doin'?'

Annie introduced him to the others

and he took a seat alongside them.

'Help yourself to coffee,' Schultz added. 'There's an empty mug.'

Usher bent forward and poured from the pot before turning to Nation. 'I hope you don't mind me askin',' he said, 'but I understand you're plannin' on ridin' to Montana.' Nation nodded. 'Well,' Usher continued, 'I was wonderin' if I could maybe ride with you.'

Nation glanced at the others. 'Why would you want to do that?' he replied. 'You've got a berth right here on the Grab All.'

'With all due respect,' Usher said, 'I reckon the time's come for me to move on and I figure I'd as soon ride with an outfit like yours as not.'

Muleskin laughed. 'Some outfit,' he chortled.

'We ain't exactly everyone's idea of a goin' concern,' Nation added.

Usher shrugged. 'Maybe you could use another hand,' he said.

Nation looked closely at him. Without his assistance, things might have turned out a whole lot worse for Annie. He could sympathize with Usher's sentiments. The time always seemed to come when it was right to make a change. He looked at Quitman and the doc. 'Any objections?' he asked.

'Nope,' Quitman said.

The doc just shook his head.

'How about you, Annie?' Nation said.

She smiled. 'How could I have any objections?' she answered.

Nation turned to Usher. 'You heard them,' he said. 'Consider yourself signed to the brand.'

Another day passed. The doc removed the bandage from Nation's hand and he spent part of the morning flexing it and practising his draw. By the time he had finished, he was satisfied that he had recovered as much of its movement as he was likely to. There was no doubt that he had lost something. Quitman was watching from the veranda.

'Even in my law-keepin' days, I was never a fast gun,' he said.

Nation looked up at him curiously.

'Is that why you handed in your badge?' he said.

Quitman shook his head. 'Nope. That wasn't it. I figured I wasn't needed any more.'

After a few moments he went back inside the ranch-house. Nation remained standing in the yard. Once again he had the feeling that there might have been something in the past between Annie and Quitman. He wondered about the reasons they all had for accompanying him on this escapade. Flexing his hand once more, he set off towards the stables to check on the horses.

* * *

The next morning, after breakfast, they made their farewells to Schultz and rode away from the Grab All. They were six in number now, Usher having joined them. Schultz had provided them with the additional information that Rackham had mentioned the name of Hooker's Bluff, but Nation knew they were in for a long ride with no guarantee that they would find their destination in a hurry. His guess was that Hooker's Bluff was some kind of landmark in the foothills of the Rockies. He had been that way before, but it was a long time ago.

They made good progress because they didn't need to be looking out for any sign. Annie's foot was better and so was Nation's hand, but he had a fresh cause of discomfort. It was the scars left by the bear when it had sunk its claws into his chest. They had been troubling him on and off for some time but the doc had assured him there was nothing to be concerned about. There was no infection. It was just a natural consequence.

'You figure it'll go away in time?' Nation asked.

Before the doc had had a chance to reply, Muleskin burst in with a tirade against bears in general. 'If my leg's anythin' to go by,' he concluded, 'you're gonna be stuck with it for life.'

'You get much pain?' Nation asked.

'I sure do. Them varmints must have

some kinda poison in their claws. One of these days I'm gonna get even.'

'The bear that got you must be long gone,' the doc said. 'How many years ago was it?'

'Not so many I'm ever likely to forget,' Muleskin replied. 'Or forgive. One bear's the same as another. I hate the whole tribe of 'em.'

The doc turned to Nation, not wanting to inflame the old-timer any further. 'It should go away,' he said. 'The pain, I mean. Let me know if it gets any worse.'

★   ★   ★

Rackham and his gang of gunslicks topped a final rise and sat their horses, gazing down on the valley below.

'Well, what do you think, boys?' Rackham said.

It was an ideal spot for a ranch and they could see scattered cattle grazing in the meadows.

'There ain't too many of 'em,' one man remarked.

'No, but there soon will be.' Rackham raised himself in his stirrups and pointed to the opposite slopes through which a narrow pass was clearly visible. 'There are ranches all round these valleys,' he said. 'The cattle are more or less runnin' free.'

The men glanced at each other and grinned.

'I think you're beginnin' to catch on,' Rackham continued. 'With a little judicial weedin' of those cattle critters, we can build us up a real big herd. Nobody's even gonna miss 'em. When we want, we can drift 'em through the ranges and sell 'em off. We're gonna make our fortunes, boys!' The men began to whoop and cheer.

'You sure got this worked out,' someone said. 'It's like the Grab All over again.'

'Exactly,' Rackham replied. 'It's a foolproof plan. It worked on the Grab All and it'll work just fine here too. The cowpokes do the graft and we enjoy the profits.'

He felt a glow of self-satisfaction. He had made his way and become a rich man. Now the final brick was about to be placed on the edifice of his ambitions with the acquisition of this new ranch in Montana. It suddenly occurred to him that he hadn't even given it a name yet. Its current title, the Block E, was too ordinary. It needed something more striking, more memorable, the sort of name that people would remember him by.

'OK,' he said when the uproar had ceased. 'Let's get on down there.'

* * *

Hooker's Bluff wasn't the name of a landmark, as Nation had surmised. It was a small settlement consisting of a few shacks and false-framed structures in the very shadow of the mountains. He and his group rode in and stopped outside a building with the name 'Missoula Bar' scrawled across it. A number of horses were fastened to the hitch-rail. Nation considered them for a few moments before dismounting to take a closer look.

'What is it?' Quitman asked.

Nation pointed at one of the horses' flanks. 'A Grab All brand,' he said. 'Looks like it's been ridden hard too. I think we might be in luck.'

Annie looked alarmed. 'You mean Denton?' she said.

The others started to dismount but Nation stopped them. 'It doesn't have to mean anythin',' he said.

'You're goin' in?' Muleskin asked.

'Sure. That's what we came for, to try and get some information about Rackham.'

'We'll come with you,' Quitman said.

Nation shook his head. 'I figure it might be a better idea if you stay out of it. We don't want to invite trouble. We need supplies. Go over to the general store. By the time you've finished I'll be right back.' They didn't look very happy with his suggestion.

'You got back-up if you need it,'

Muleskin concluded. Without waiting further, Nation turned away and stepped through the batwing doors.

Inside, the place was hazy with smoke. A few people sat around at tables but Nation's eyes were drawn to a group at the bar. They were dusty-looking and begrimed as if they had come a long way. He was aware that eyes were on him as he strode slowly across the room. The bartender was standing at one end of the bar and glanced up idly at Nation's approach.

'Whiskey,' Nation said.

The barman glanced at the men standing next to Nation and then poured a drink from a bottle behind the counter. Nation put one foot up on the bar rail and looked in the mirror. Two men who had been sitting at a nearby table had changed position slightly; just enough to allow their gun hands freer movement. The men at the bar had also fanned out.

'I noticed that one of the horses outside carried a Grab All brand,' he said. 'Whose horse is it?'

There was no reply. One of the men now standing towards the edge of the bar licked his lips.

'Thing is, I just rode from over that way. I'm lookin' for a man called Rackham. He owns the Grab All but right now I got reason to believe he's up here lookin' at another spread.'

Again, his words were greeted with silence till the barman spoke. 'Nobody here knows anythin' about a man called Rackham,' he said.

'You speak for everybody?' Nation replied.

The man at the end of the bar looked across at him. 'Who's askin'?' he said.

'The name's Nation. Now, I'd be willin' to bet that you go by the handle of Denton.'

It was little more than a shot in the dark, but Nation wasn't slow to observe the expression which suddenly passed across the man's face. If he didn't know Nation by sight, he knew now who it was confronting him. At the same instant of recognition, Nation saw movement behind him from the men at the table and spun round as a shot flew past him, exploding the bottles behind the bar in a shower of splintering glass. Nation's finger squeezed the trigger of his .44 and one of the men went staggering back as a bullet smashed into his chest. In the same movement Nation adjusted his position and sent another slug slamming into the second man. He flung out an arm as he fired and sent a bullet thudding into the ceiling. Above the crashing sound of the guns Nation heard a voice shouting: 'Watch out!'

Instinctively, he dived for the floor, just as a bullet from Denton singed his cheek. He heard a loud detonation from the back of the saloon. Denton went reeling back, blood oozing from his stomach. Another shot blasted out; for a few seconds Denton clung to the bar and then he slithered sideways, ending up in a crumpled heap in the sawdust. Nation looked toward the batwings to see Usher standing there with a smoking gun. The batwings flew open again and Quitman burst through with his revolver drawn.

'Nation, you OK?' he shouted.

Nation got to his feet. He felt blood running down his face and put his hand up to feel his wound.

'It's just a graze,' he called. 'It musta been a mighty close thing.'

Usher and Quitman came forward. Quitman bent over the two men Nation had shot and then looked up, shaking his head. Nation was already kneeling beside Denton.

'He's dead,' he muttered. He stood up again and turned to the barman. 'You saw what happened,' he said. 'Those varmints were the first to draw.'

The barman looked from Nation to Usher to Quitman. 'Sure,' he said, 'it was self-defence.'

Nation approached the bar and leaned against it. 'Now, like I was sayin', I'm lookin' for a man called Rackham. I figure those gunhawks were lookin' for him too and maybe let somethin' slip about where he is.'

The bartender hesitated. 'They mentioned somethin',' he said.

'Yeah?'

The bartender still seemed reluctant to talk. Nation couldn't work out whether he was frightened or whether he just didn't trust strangers.

'Look,' he said eventually, 'I never heard of this Rackham *hombre* before those boys blew into town. They said he was the new owner of a ranch up in the hills. That's all I know.'

'There must be somethin' else.'

'Why don't you try askin' Lou Peters?' he said. 'He's an attorney. He handles any real estate issues round these parts. If Rackham has bought up some property, he would know.'

Nation nodded and turned away. As an afterthought, he stepped back and drained his glass of whiskey. He placed some bills on the table in payment. 'What's left outa that should pay for any damage,' he said, 'and you'd better send somebody for the undertaker.'

A bystander got to his feet.

'I'll go,' he said.

Nation turned and walked through the saloon, accompanied by Usher and Quitman. As they stepped through the batwing doors they were met by Muleskin and a flustered Annie.

'What's happening?' she gasped. 'We heard shots. Is anybody hurt?'

'She would have got here a lot quicker but I kinda slowed her down,' Muleskin said.

Annie noticed for the first time that Nation was bleeding. Before she could ask a further question, Quitman reassured her.

'Everyone's fine,' he said. 'Nation's face is grazed, nothin' more. It seems like he encountered a little difficulty extracting the information we wanted.' Annie looked blankly at them.

'You were right,' Nation said. 'It was Denton in there, together with a few of his friends. We won't have to worry about him any more.' Annie was about to say something but Nation forestalled her. 'Did you get those things we needed?' he said.

Muleskin nodded. 'Yup. We got everythin'.'

'So now we know where to find Rackham,' Nation said, 'what are we waitin' for?'

They were about to climb into leather when the batwings flew open behind them and a man emerged. With a brief nod in their direction he mounted one of the horses tied at the hitch-rail and rode off. At the same moment they saw a figure approaching. It was the marshal.

'Hold it!' he said. 'Wait right there.'

The marshal came up to them and then carried on into the saloon; they waited for him to come out again. When he did he was accompanied by the bartender and two of his customers. He looked closely at them, reserving his longest look for Annie.

'There are three men dead in there,' he said.

'I never provoked them,' Nation

replied. 'Anythin' that happened in there was in self-defence.' He faced the barman and the men accompanying him. 'Ask these folk. They saw it all.'

The marshal did not reply but glanced down the street. A wagon pulled by a black horse with a plume on its head was already approaching.

'Here comes the undertaker,' the marshal commented. He turned back to Nation. 'I hear you were makin' queries about someone called Rackham.'

'That's right. We understand he's bought a ranch up in the hills. The bartender here suggested we ask somebody called — what was it?'

The bartender was about to reply but the marshal spoke for him. 'Try the Block E,' he said. 'The former owner is an acquaintance of mine. Seems he sold up to some rancher from Wyoming. Guess he could be your man.'

'Thanks. Sure appreciate the information.'

'Just make sure you never set foot in Hooker's Bluff again,' the marshal said.

Muleskin spat into the dust. 'It sure don't come across as a right friendly sort of place,' he said.

Nation put one foot in a stirrup and stepped into leather. 'Thanks for your help, Marshal,' he said. He touched his spurs to the roan's flanks and began to ride, followed by the others. Only when they had left the town behind and were heading for the mountains did he think of the man who had left the saloon while they were involved with the marshal and ridden away in the same direction.

* * *

After everything that had happened in Hooker's Bluff, it was a relief to make camp that evening and take time to recuperate, so it was quite late the following morning when they set out. They were climbing higher and Annie reckoned that they must have gone wrong. The terrain just seemed unsuitable for ranching but Nation and

173

Muleskin knew better. Every valley was a natural enclosure where cattle could be raised protected by high cliffs. There was plenty of water and good grass. Rackham was no fool. He must have planned his every move with careful attention since the days he had ridden the lines on the Forty-Five.

Nation continued to lead the way. He knew they were close to their target and when he rounded a bend of the trail, he had his first view of Rackham's ranch in the valley beneath. Drawing to a stop, he reached for his field glasses. The ranch-house looked solid. It was built of logs and there were a number of substantial buildings behind it. He expected to see signs of activity but though he searched closely, he could see none. Behind the ranch-house but still some distance away a butte towered hundreds of feet into the air; it was Nation's guess that whoever had built the ranch-house had chosen the site because water would be found at its base.

'There it is,' he said, handing the

glasses to Muleskin, who took a long look.

'I don't like it,' he said. 'There should be somebody around.' He put the glasses back to his eyes and swept the valley. 'Plenty of cattle,' he said, 'and there's a few people watchin' 'em.' He passed the glasses to the others.

'We've still some distance to go,' Nation said.

'What are we gonna do?' Quitman asked. 'Ride right on in?'

'I'm thinkin' it over,' Nation said.

They began to move on down the trail. It took another bend and they temporarily lost sight of the ranch-house. They were descending towards the valley floor and had to go slowly because of the incline, the horses picking their way with delicate steps. One side of the trail fell away gradually and the other was overhung by a high, tree-covered slope.

Suddenly, far up the slope, a stone rattled. Instantly Nation's glance swept the hill. He saw a glint of light.

'Drop down!' he shouted, leaping from the saddle as he did so. He made for Annie's horse and half-assisted, half-pulled her from the startled beast as a fusillade of shots rang out from overhead, reverberating among the rocks and crags. Dragging Annie with him, he made for the shelter of the trees. The others hadn't needed a second warning and as he tumbled into the undergrowth he saw that they had sought cover too on either side of the trail.

'Sorry about that, Miss Annie,' he said. 'There was no time for niceties.'

Annie ducked down as bullets crashed into the trees over their heads.

'Don't think anything of it, Mr Nation,' she replied.

Nation looked down at her and was surprised to see the hint of a smile on her face. She certainly wasn't giving any indication of fear. 'I think we're OK here for the moment,' he said.

'You aren't going to leave me, I hope?' she replied. There was an almost winsome note in her voice.

'I need to get to my horse,' he said. 'It's bolted and taken my rifle with it.'

The horses had scattered but Nation could see three of them further back along the trail down which they had come.

'I'm going to make my way through the trees,' he said. 'You wait here and stay concealed.'

Bullets were still whipping the branches of the trees but they didn't carry much threat. Nation realized that the accidental dislodging of the pebble had probably saved their lives. It could only be Rackham up there on the hillside, but how had he been warned of their arrival?

Quickly, Nation slipped away. The barrage of fire had dwindled but it was clear from the direction of the noise that Rackham's fire was being returned. At least some of the others must have retained their rifles. He was soon abreast of the horses but they were standing in the middle of the trail and he would need to expose himself to the enemy. He made a quick calculation. With any luck, he should be just out of range. On the other hand, he might have got it wrong or some of Rackham's men might also have shifted position.

Taking a deep breath, he dashed out of the cover of the trees. Almost immediately a fresh barrage of fire exploded from the hillside, some of the bullets tearing up dirt not far from him. One of the horses started to rear at his approach and the other two shifted position, edging nervously sideways. He grabbed the reins of the nearest one and deftly removed the rifle from its scabbard. He turned to the other and did the same, but as he lifted the weapon from its sheath the horse uttered a loud bray and sank down, blood pouring from its neck. The other two horses took off, galloping away down the track. Bullets were thudding into the earth all around him now and he took advantage of the dying horse to give him some protection.

Suddenly he heard someone shouting his name; the bushes on the opposite side of the trail parted and Muleskin appeared.

'Here, take this and give me cover!' Nation shouted.

He flung the Winchester to the old-timer, who grabbed it out of the air. He looked at Nation and Nation nodded. Immediately the old-timer began to pump lead as Nation took to his heels and sprinted back across the road and into the trees. Shots were still ringing out but they posed no real threat. Now he had the rifle, he intended climbing the mountain and getting behind Rackham.

Once Nation had vanished into the undergrowth, Muleskin weighed up his situation. He was confident that Usher, Quitman and the doc had all escaped serious injury. He could hear the sounds of their guns as they responded to the fusillade that was being rained down on them. For a few moments he allowed himself to think about the dog.

He didn't know what had become of Midway but there was nothing to be done for the moment. Suddenly he had an idea. If he could make it to the ranch-house, he could create a diversion by starting a fire.

The thought no sooner entered his mind than he acted on it. He began to slither down the slope which led down into the valley. As he got lower the ranch-house came into view and he realized that it wasn't as far as he had imagined. The trail they had been riding took a switchback course down the mountain, but he was taking the most direct route. It was steep; a reasonably active man would not find it a problem but his damaged leg hampered him badly. Still, he was going quite well till his foot caught on an outcrop of rock and he went tumbling head over heels down the mountainside. The rifle which Nation had thrown to him was wrenched from his grip as his headlong fall was brought to a halt by a clump of bushes. For a moment he lay half stunned; his leg hurt a lot and he felt sore all over. Gritting his teeth, he made a big effort to struggle back to his feet. He wasn't too far from the valley floor and he began the descent once more. It seemed to take an age, but finally he was down from the mountain.

From his position, Quitman could see Usher but he had no idea what had happened to the doc. They were both directing their fire at the mountain where the gunnies were concealed, but he was aware they were probably not doing much damage. By the same token, neither were the gunslicks. For the moment, they seemed to have reached a kind of stalemate, but he didn't know how long they would be able to keep it that way. He was getting low on ammunition. The shooting had grown sporadic and he was on the alert for any change of tactic on Rackham's part.

He glanced over his shoulder. From where he lay, he could just see a corner of the ranch-house and part of a corral behind it. Suddenly he tensed. A thin plume of smoke was rising over the tops of the trees. At first he thought it must be coming from the chimney but as he watched it grew denser. He still couldn't work out what it could be; maybe Rackham or his men were up to something. Then he saw a flicker of flame and he realized that the ranch-house was on fire. He wasn't sure what to make of it, but he couldn't prevent a thin smile coming to his lips. Whatever was going on, it wasn't doing Rackham any good. He realized that the gunfire from the mountainside had ceased. Rackham's men must have seen the fire too. Could they have abandoned their position and be making their way back to the ranch-house? He looked towards Usher. The man had got to his feet and was working his way towards him.

'Somethin's happenin' down there!' he shouted as he got closer.

'Yeah. But what?'

'I don't know, but it sure seems to have distracted Rackham.' He stopped, struck by another thought. 'Say,' he said, 'you ain't seen what happened to the doc or Muleskin?'

'Muleskin was here a while back. I didn't see him move.'

They both looked about. The mountainside was quiet. A dark cloud of smoke was blowing towards them and they could hear the crackling of flames.

'Come on,' Quitman said. 'Let's get up the mountain and see if we can take those buzzards by surprise.'

* * *

Once Nation and his little group had been warned of the ambush he had so carefully prepared, Rackham realized that he had a fight on his hands. He cursed the fact that something had happened to give him away. However, there were only six people in Nation's party, and one of them was a woman, so he didn't have any real doubts about the outcome. Then he saw the smoke rising from his newly acquired ranch-house and his attitude changed. Somehow, fate seemed to be against him.

Just when his plans had seemed about to come to fruition, this man Nation had appeared from nowhere. It had seemed a simple matter to get rid of him and the potential danger he represented, but one way and another Gunter had failed him and Nation had survived. He had been brought the news of Nation's arrival in Hooker's Bluff by someone who had been present at the shoot-out there between Nation and Denton. It seemed his luck was still in. To bushwhack Nation and be finally rid of him had seemed a relatively simple matter. Now that too had failed. He watched as the flames from the burning ranch-house rose higher above the trees.

'Let's get movin'!' he shouted. 'The varmints must have got away and set fire to the ranch.'

The gunnies loosed off a fresh salvo of gunfire before drifting away through the trees to get back to their horses.

* * *

When he was confident that the blaze he had started had taken hold, Muleskin hobbled away from the ranch-house. His leg was giving him a lot of pain and he felt weak. His tumble down the mountainside had taken more out of him than he had realized. He staggered towards the corral but before he reached it his legs gave way beneath him and he sank to the ground. He managed to rise and limp on a few more steps before his legs buckled again and he fell awkwardly. He dragged himself a little further till he was able to prop his back up against a fence post. From this position he looked back at the burning building.

Dense, acrid smoke was now billowing from it. Some of it was coming in his direction and he began to cough and splutter as it took hold of his lungs. He continued to stare as the first tongues of flame began to spiral from the building like glowing serpents. As he watched something more terrible seemed to emerge, something thick and ghastly and monstrous. He had slid down and as he struggled to sit upright the dark, amorphous mass began to assume a more definite shape, to congeal and then solidify into the form and substance of a huge black bear. Terror gripped him as he vaguely reached for the rifle which Nation had thrown him; then he remembered he had lost it in his fall. Fear was engulfing him, robbing him of his senses, but he retained enough of them to reach for the six-gun which he had stuck in his belt. As the bear drew near, he pulled it out and fired. The hammer fell on an empty chamber. In a last agony of desperation he hurled the useless lump of iron in the monster's face. The effort of doing it made him fall back and his head banged against the fence post. There was no escape. The bear was upon him and as he opened his mouth in a soundless scream the bear's fierce, foaming visage seemed to melt, to dissolve and transform into a face, a familiar face which he recognized as the doc's.

'Hurley?' he managed to say.

'Yes. Who did you think it was?' the doc replied.

Muleskin felt confused. 'Good boy, Midway,' he said. He closed his eyes and then, after a few moments, opened them again. His head felt slightly clearer. 'What happened to the dog?' he said.

'The dog's fine,' Hurley replied. 'Just take it easy. Everything's fine.'

★　★　★

Rackham and his gang of gunslingers quickly made their way through the trees towards the open space where they had left their horses. As he cleared the last of the pines, Rackham stopped and gaped, his jaw falling open.

'What the hell!' he muttered. 'Where are the horses?'

His men, coming up behind him, looked around the glade with puzzled expressions. 'Are you sure we got the right place?' one of them said. 'These clearings all look the same.'

Rackham rounded on him. 'Do you think I'm stupid?' he snapped. The man shrank back. 'Take a look around,' Rackham ordered. The men were about to split up to carry out his bidding when a voice behind them rang out.

'No need! The horses are gone. We got our rifles trained right on you so I suggest you drop your weapons and do it real slow.'

Rackham half-turned as one man's hand dropped towards his gunbelt. Nation squeezed the trigger of the Winchester and sent a shot winging through the air close to the man's head.

'I wouldn't try that again!' he rapped. 'Rackham, tell your men to follow instructions or the next one is for you.'

Rackham hesitated but the sound of Nation levering his rifle brought him to a decision. 'Do as he says,' he concluded. The men obeyed his command and, when they had done so, Nation stepped out of cover. From another position, Quitman and Usher emerged into the open with their six-guns in their hands.

'The game's over, Rackham,' Nation said. 'As for the rest of you, I'll give you a choice. You either clear out of here or you accompany Rackham to the nearest jailhouse.'

The men looked at each other. 'What about our horses?' one of them said.

'Nothin' doing,' Nation replied. 'If you start walkin', you should make it to Hooker's Bluff. Eventually.' The men grumbled and one of them muttered an oath beneath his breath.

'It's up to you,' Nation said. 'But remember this. There isn't gonna be much left of that ranch for any of you to go back to. Rackham's time is through. Best you move on and don't ever come back.'

The gunmen still hesitated but eventually one of them moved away and the others began to follow. Seeing them give way, Rackham started to plead with them but his words soon became a torrent of abuse.

'You can see what Rackham really thinks about you,' Nation said. 'Keep walkin' and give my regards to the marshal when you get to Hooker's Bluff.' In a few more seconds the glade was deserted except for Rackham and his captors.

'OK,' Nation said. 'I think it's time we took a look at what's left of your ranch-house.'

Once they had reunited and rounded up the horses, Nation and his companions wasted no time in leaving the smouldering ruin of the old Block E behind them. It was a long ride back to Wyoming and they would have to put up with Rackham and his complaining and cursing all the way. Nation had considered returning to Hooker's Bluff with him but decided against it. He had no wish to renew acquaintance with the marshal there and he didn't want to run into any of Rackham's gunslicks.

★ ★ ★

They had set up camp on the second evening after their departure. The mountains were well behind them. A cold wind blew but they felt comfortable by the roaring flames of the camp fire.

'You know,' Muleskin said, 'I'm kinda disappointed our little adventure is almost over.'

'I feel the same way as you, Muleskin,' Annie said. 'I reckon I'm going to be sorry when we get back to Gunsight.' They sank into silence for a while till eventually Nation spoke.

'If you don't like the idea of pickin' things up again in Gunsight,' he said, 'you don't have to.'

'What do you mean?' Muleskin said.

'Well, I hope you haven't forgotten that I'm now the owner of the Forty-Five. That place has been allowed to go to ruin. I reckon it's gonna take a whole lot of hard graft to get it up and runnin' again.'

'You're going to attempt to make a go of the old Forty-Five?' the doc put in.

'Figure I'd give it a try,' Nation answered. 'But there's no way I can do it on my own.' The others looked at each other.

'Hell!' Muleskin cried. 'It looks like you got yourself a whole outfit. From now on, we're all ridin' for the Forty-Five.'

The night wore on and they remained sitting by the fire, each thinking of the future. From time to time one of them would rise to throw another branch on the fire. The wind whipped up and outside the circle of flames the horses stamped. Midway got to his feet and uttered a growl.

'It's only the wind, old fella,' Muleskin said. 'It ain't no bear.' Doc Hurley looked at him with a certain degree of apprehension written on his face.

'It's OK, Doc,' Muleskin said. He faced the others. 'I had a bit of a turn back there after I set the ranch on fire,' he said. 'The doc knows. Somehow I got confused and thought he was some kind of big bear comin' to get me. Right afterwards, when you folk started comin' back, I felt altogether different. I don't know what it was, but I feel as though some kinda weight's been lifted off my back.'

'That's good,' Nation said. 'You sure seemed to get riled whenever you mentioned it.'

'Yeah, I guess so. But there was more to it than that.'

Annie made a move towards the old-timer. 'You don't have to go into it again,' she said.

Muleskin turned to Quitman. 'You have no cause to blame yourself either,' he said. Without waiting for Quitman to respond, he addressed Nation. 'I think we owe you an explanation. Now that we're workin' for you, I reckon it's good that it's all come out into the open.'

He paused, looking at Quitman. 'I'm sorry,' he said. 'I hope you don't mind.'

'Go ahead,' said Quitman. 'I've gone over it all so many times, it's almost a relief.'

'It was like this,' Muleskin resumed. 'I got tangled up with that goddamn bear when it attacked Miss Annie. We were out ridin' and we'd stopped to rest the horses. The varmint came out of nowhere.' He hesitated.

'It's OK, Muleskin,' Quitman said. 'The thing is, Nation, I was there too and when that bear appeared, I guess I just froze. Me and Miss Annie, we had a sort of understanding. I felt ashamed . . .'

'None of it was your fault,' Annie intervened. 'There was no need for you to blame yourself.'

'I guess I can see that now,' Quitman said. 'But it was different then.'

'That was when Quitman handed in his badge and left Gunsight to live away from town,' Muleskin concluded. 'I guess in a way Annie quit too. I was in a bad way for a while. She looked after me and then she offered me a place to stay. And that's the way things were till you rode into town.'

He stopped and they lapsed into silence. Nation rose and walked over to the horses. He came back carrying a flask in his hand.

'What you got there?' the doc asked.

'Call it medicine,' Nation said. 'Just don't take too much at a time.'

He opened the flask and took a swig before handing it to Annie. 'Like I say, take it real easy,' he said. She swallowed and then gasped. Quitman took the flask and drank from it before handing it to Usher, who finally passed it to the doc.

'Hell, I see what you mean,' the doc said. 'What is that stuff?'

Muleskin grinned sheepishly. 'It's my own concoction,' he said. Just then they heard muttering coming from a little distance away. Muleskin rose and handed the flask to Rackham. He took a swallow and then burst out spluttering as Muleskin rejoined the others.

'I didn't like to deprive him,' he said. 'That should shut him up till we hit Gunsight.'

The others laughed and Midway began to bark.

Muleskin patted his head and he quieted down again.

'Looks like the old fella's volunteerin' to act shotgun on Rackham the rest of the way,' Muleskin said. 'Guess he's joined the outfit too.'

THE END

We do hope that you have enjoyed reading this large print book.

Did you know that all of our titles are available for purchase?

We publish a wide range of high quality large print books including:
Romances, Mysteries, Classics General Fiction Non Fiction and Westerns

Special interest titles available in large print are:
The Little Oxford Dictionary Music Book, Song Book Hymn Book, Service Book

Also available from us courtesy of Oxford University Press:
Young Readers' Dictionary (large print edition) Young Readers' Thesaurus (large print edition)

For further information or a free brochure, please contact us at:
Ulverscroft Large Print Books Ltd., The Green, Bradgate Road, Anstey, Leicester, LE7 7FU, England.
Tel: (00 44) **0116 236 4325**
Fax: (00 44) **0116 234 0205**

CROOKED CREEK

Greg Mitchell

Raiders are terrorizing the buffalo range, wiping out hunters' camps. 'Notso' Wise, a former Texas Ranger, is recruited to bring the thieves to justice. Doubts exist that the local lawmen are pursuing the raiders with sufficient vigour, and Notso doubts he has the subtlety the job requires. The raiders are led by Jim Hardiman, a ruthless villain who uses a network of informers, backed up by cold-blooded murder. Has Notso got what it takes to bring him down?

LAST DAY IN PARADISE

Paul Green

When professional gambler Jimmy 'the Kid' Casey beats the son of wealthy ranch owner Jack Hartigan in a game of poker, he is forced to shoot the young man dead in self-defence. Hartigan vows revenge and the card player flees the town of Paradise, only to find himself pursued by a gang of killers led by Abe Morgan. Things become more complicated when the gang captures Jimmy's fiancée, and renegade Apaches go on the warpath.

DRIFTER

Steve Hayes

When El Carnicero and his gang raid the Mercer ranch, they turn life upside-down for young Emily. A man known as Drifter is an old friend of the Mercers and wants to get back at the gang, who have fled to Mexico, despite being outgunned. However, he hasn't counted on the help of Emily, who is determined to retrieve the horses the gang stole — especially her beloved Diablo. Also joined by an old lawman and Mesquite Jennings, they ride off in search of justice.

A THUNDER OF GUNS

Clay Starmer

For Jeb Sullivan, racked with despair over the deaths of his wife and child, there seems little to live for. He seeks to join his lost love in the afterlife, challenging any thug he meets to achieve this. But his arrival in Driftwood changes everything, and he soon falls in love with TJ Griffin. Accepting the sheriff's badge, he has a daily battle to stay alive in this lawless corner of the West when a tinderbox of tensions flashes into war.